"He'll be here. "He'll be here."   She chanted this in her head over and over like a mantra as she fussed over the spread she had prepared for the day's gathering.   As usual, she had made enough food to feed a small army, yet she looked around and wondered if there would be enough.   Trays of fresh vegetables and homemade dips, creamy cheeses and fresh baked breads, stuffed calamata olives with rye crackers and smoked salmon spread, fresh strawberry and melon salad with mint, German potato salad, and several assorted pastries adorned what Effie dubbed "the

appetizer table". The cold items all in shiny stainless steel bowls and plates sat relaxing in pans of ice. On a day this hot, everyone had contemplated how nice it would be to wade in a giant pan of ice. Everyone but Effie. The blood in Effie's veins ran as cold as the ice itself. "I don't know if I can do this," she thought as she nervously watched the dirt road for any sign of him. Effie's greatest support and comfort seemed to always come from the one person who seemed the least capable of supporting anyone or anything, much less himself. Time after time she had bailed him out of mess after mess, and yet had always regarded him as her best friend in all the world. She badly needed him here today. She needed to draw strength from his presence. She had serious doubts about the "bomb" she was going to drop on her family today, but she knew once she saw his face, she would remember why it had to be done. Most of all, she needed to know that no matter what, he would be okay.

"Mother, honest to God! We are all melting up here waiting. Can't we go down by the lake, in the shade? It's bad enough that nobody has eaten, since this shin dig was supposed to start at twelve-thirty." Sissy's face was red as an apple, partially from the heat of the day, and partially from anger. Effie surveyed the faces of the others, who all seemed to silently agree with Sissy, although none of them seemed quite as adamant as she. It was now two o'clock, which meant Jacob was an hour and a half late.

"That's really not late for Jacob," Effie thought to herself, and for an instant a smirk formed on her lips. "Alright gang, I guess it'd be okay if we went down by the lake in the shade. We'll eat soon, I promise. Marcus, you're still up to the challenge, right?" Ever since David had died five years ago, Effie's son-in-law had been the official master of the grill.

"Always mom," Marcus replied and flashed a smile that was as warm and genuine as always.

The lake property was gorgeous, quiet, secluded from the world it seemed. The upper portion of the lot was where the camper and tables were placed. Dining and sleeping were usually confined to this area. Several hundred feet down a steep incline was the lower portion of the lot. It was smaller, shady, and bordered the crystal clear lake. The dock invited everyone to jump in for a swim or bask in the sun, while the nearby rowboats and canoes called out to those who liked to fish or go for a relaxing tour of the lake. David and Effie had been given the property as a wedding gift from his parents after they married. "The only decent thing they ever did for me," Effie was fond of saying. As newlyweds they would often camp here in the summer, frolicking in the sun like teenagers, making love on the grass in the moonlight. As the children came along and grew, their romantic retreat transformed into a family getaway. It seemed that in the summer, the family of five spent more time at the lake property than they did at home.

Effie glanced around pensively at her small gathering of people. Sissy and her formidable husband Jeff Carlisle sat talking stiffly and drinking chardonnay. With everyone now settled in the shade down by the lake, Sissy's temper seemed to have waned a bit.   Margo and her husband, Marcus Bellows, sat on the dock, feet dangling in the water.   Marcus was rubbing Margo's swollen belly which contained Effie's first grandchild.   Sam "Clarkie" Clark, who had been David's best friend, confidant, and lawyer, was bird watching with a set of binoculars. When all was said and done, there would be seven people at the lake that day. "Seven is supposed to be lucky," Effie thought, "God, I hope so."   She didn't really believe in luck, she was a God fearing woman, never missed church on Sunday, and was known in the community as a prayer warrior.

Effie swallowed hard, she had been feeling nauseated all day. She couldn't remember the last time she'd had a full night's rest, or the last time she took any pleasure in eating. The weight and worry of a lifetime of secrets were taking a toll on her. While David had been the head of the family, Effie had always been the heart. She felt things deeply, too deeply, and often made herself sick with worry. Jacob, a drinker, drifter, and somewhat of a schemer, was often responsible for keeping her up all night. Nobody quite understood the bond that Effie had with Jacob, and sometimes she questioned it herself. "But then again," Effie reasoned, "nobody really knows who I am." Finally, in the distance Effie heard the rumble of an engine, and looked up to see a rust bucket of a car pull into the drive, way too fast, spewing a cloud of dust and smoke.   Jacob had arrived. "Let the games begin," Effie thought as she slowly made her way up the incline to greet her youngest child.

Chapter 2

"Oh honey, your hair is so long!" Effie embraced her son with the kind of hug one would give to a loved one going off to war. She had just seen him the month before, but if she had her way about it, Jacob would move back home with her and never leave again. He had, in fact, moved in and out of Effie's house so many times that the neighbors thought he did actually live there. "Hi there Mama," Jacob breathed into her ear all the while eyeballing the bottle of beer he was clutching in his right hand.

The rest of the gathering made their way up the incline, knowing that if they didn't at least act cordial, it would ruin Effie's mood for the day. Marcus shot a quick nod and wave to Jacob, who was still being crushed against Effie's ample bosom, before wandering over to the grill and fire pit to light them. "Goddam it Jacob, were you drinking that beer while you were driving??" Sissy's face was apple red again. "Language, Clarissa," Effie snapped as if she was scolding a toddler. The only person who ever used Sissy's real name was her mother, and usually at times like these when she was angry or annoyed with her. She had been dubbed "Sissy" when Margo was born, at it had stuck. "I mean, really mother? This idiot lives like a frat boy, which is odd since he never bothered to finish college.   Who in their right mind drives around in the middle of the day drinking a goddam beer??"   Effie finally released Jacob from her arms, steam rolling out of her ears.   "Clarissa, you are not at all too old, or too big for me to slap your jaws for you!   Bite your filthy tongue or go cool off in the lake or something!" Sissy pouted and lowered her head for a moment before returning an angry, squinted look in Jacob's direction.

Effie did not appreciate coarse language, and all three of her children knew that.

She had grown up in the strictest of homes and had been taught impeccable manners.   It wasn't a very warm upbringing, and hugs and praise were few and far between, but Effie had been taught a level of decorum that she had hoped to pass on to her own children. She had also vowed that unlike she, they would be loved, and know they were loved as long as she lived.

"Margo!   My God, you're huge!"   Jacob made his way to her and embraced her warmly.   Margo had the sweetest spirit Jacob had ever encountered, and despite all of his shenanigans, the two had always been close.   "I'm counting the days," Margo said as she wiped beads of sweat from her forehead.   Despite having to deal with being in her third trimester during the heat of the summer, Margo had enjoyed every minute of her pregnancy.   It seemed to Marcus that the bigger she got, the happier she became.

  Clarkie extended a plump hand in Jacob's direction, and then turned the hand shake into a hug.   "Jacob my boy, it's nice to see you!   It's always nice to see you casually, and not just when I'm bailing you out of trouble!" Clarkie was smiling and winking, so it was hard for Jacob to be sore about his statement. "Thanks Clarkie! Gee whiz, you're about the same size as Margo! When are you due?" Both men laughed heartily as Sissy and Jeff rolled their eyes in the background. Clarkie joked, "It's not fair though, Margo hasn't lost her hair with the growth of her belly like I have!"

With Marcus still manning the grill and everyone else chattering away, Effie stole off to the camper for a moment. The old camper was always kept immaculately clean, yet it had a very distinctive smell about it. The smell was slightly oceanic, from the lake breezes, mixed with wood smoke from their many camp fires, and a hint of cedar from the drawers. It was a smell that brought floods of memories to Effie's mind every time she opened the door. On this particular day, there were several boxes placed about the camper that weren't normally there. Effie had wondered if Sissy or Margo would question her about the boxes when they had come to the camper to use the facilities, but neither girl had said a word. At the top of the box closest to the door was what Effie had come for - her expensive camera and a black bag with lenses and filters for it. Effie was wild about photography, and to the chagrin of her children, every gathering or special occasion had to be extensively photographed. "Today will be different," she thought, "these pictures will be for them this time, not me."

Effie's hands were wet with sweat. She wiped them on her plaid apron, and smoothed her dark curls behind her ears. She had maintained the same hairdo for as long as she could remember, only nowadays, there was a touch of silver at the temples. Clarkie, would you be so sweet as to take a couple of pictures of us for me?" Without waiting for a proper response, Effie shoved the camera in Clarkie's direction. "C'mon kids, we'll stand at the top of the incline with our backs to the lake. It'll be beautiful!" The three Banks children shuffled to their place with the same enthusiasm as an inmate to the gas chamber. "Marcus, Jeff, I want you guys over here too." Effie paused before lining up for the picture to study her three children, and two son-in- laws standing in the sun.

Sissy at 5'10" tall had acquired most of her surprisingly waspy features from the Banks side.   With long, straight copper hair, clear green eyes, high cheek bones, a button nose, and skin the color of fresh oats, she was quite a beauty.   "If she were only a happier person…" Effie let her thoughts wander for a moment. Sissy and Jeff had been trying for quite some time to have a family.   Effie had often thought that Jeff, with his blonde haired, blue eyed, Apollo like appearance, would make gorgeous children with Sissy.

Sweet Margo was two inches shorter than Sissy, and not as classically beautiful.   With hazel eyes, wavy chestnut hair (which she always kept short), sepia skin, full lips, and a prominent nose, she, out of all three of them, was probably the most equal blend of her parent's genetics.   She had the "glow" that people talk about when women are expecting.   Effie was over the moon about the pregnancy, but sometimes imagined that their child would be born with a book in his hand. Margo's husband Marcus, with unkempt black hair, and wire rimmed glasses, looked more like an English librarian than an Irish Catholic from North Carolina.

Jacob, at 6'5", looked like Effie's vision of an Old Testament Hebrew. He had inherited Effie's espresso colored hair with natural loose curls, dark brown eyes, sharp hooked nose, olive skin, and cleft chin. He had a perpetual five o'clock shadow that Effie had long ago given up on trying to get him to shave. He had taken to letting his hair grow shoulder length, which Effie would fuss about, but would secretly think to herself that it suited him perfectly. "If only he'd find the right girl," Effie thought. She cleared her head, deciding that it was time to stand with her family for the pictures.

Effie stood in the middle, Jacob who was a good foot and a half taller, stood behind her and wrapped his arms around her. On her right was Margo with Marcus in tow, on her left Sissy and Jeff.

"Beautiful," Clarkie exclaimed sincerely as he started snapping pictures. He knew Effie wouldn't be satisfied with one or two shots. After what seemed like an eternity to the young people, Effie changed things up. "Kids, I want some shots of just the three of you. Marcus, Jeff, you fellas don't mind, do you?" Both shook their heads and were silently relieved to be able to go about their previous activities, Marcus fussing over the grill, and Jeff drinking wine and reading his newspaper. "Left to right in birth order would be nice I think," Effie chirped and stood back to watch her brood line up.   They were all beautiful she thought, and although one could clearly see they were closely related, it amazed her how different they were from one another.

"Alright kids, I know it's hot out here, but lets see if we can make your mother a happy woman, and get some really nice shots of the three of you."   Clarkie was doing his level best to be a cheerleader, thinking that maybe his enthusiasm would break through the wall of ice that was surrounding Sissy.   He posed the three of them over and over, in different order and position, taking several shots each time.   Clarkie wanted, no, he NEEDED these pictures to be perfect.   He had always done everything in his power to please Effie, but he knew this time things were different.   These pictures weren't really for Effie, they were for all of them. These would be more than just pictures, these would be a glimpse at a moment in time when things were familiar and safe. Clarkie knew that there was a hurricane brewing that would strip this family bare to the bones.

Chapter 3

By the time everyone sat down to eat, it was nearly dinner time. Effie knew that if she had set the time for half past noon, in reality it would turn into a dinner instead of a lunch, and she was fine with that. With the amount of food she had prepared for the "appetizer table", everyone had eaten lunch anyway.

"Marcus, you've done a fantastic job on the grill! Everything looks wonderful!"

Effie was clearly fond of her newest son-in-law, and felt more as if he were her own child.   She had had multiple arguments with Sissy over the last two years about not being as close to Jeff. One particular day when she had had her fill of Sissy's argumentative tone on the phone, she had said to her, "Clarissa, you don't seem particularly fond of your husband most of the time, so why on earth should I?"   Sissy brooded over this conversation for a week or so, and then just like every other conflict that occurred in the family, it was swept under the rug and never mentioned again.   Bitterness and unforgiveness were the bread and butter of the family, while jealousy was the house wine.   Effie's prayer was that when the oncoming storm swept through this family the negativity would be washed out to sea, leaving room in their hearts only for the love that they had all buried in some way or another.   "Heal this family Lord," Effie had prayed over and over in her head.

 "I'm so glad that we could all get together like this," Margo beamed. Somehow Margo always found the silver lining in any given situation.   It didn't matter to her that Sissy was acting like this was the last place on earth that she wanted to be, or that Jacob was already more than halfway through a twelve pack of beer, she was just happy that they were all together.   The last time they were all together in one place had been five years before when their father died. Margo was hopeful that this would be a happier time for them.

"Does everyone have what they need?" Effie didn't bother to wait for an answer. "Sissy, I'd like for you to return thanks for the meal please."   Sissy frowned and gave a sideways glance to her husband. "Mother, you know I don't believe in that nonsense."   Effie sighed aloud.   With what she knew was about to happen to the family she decided she would pick her battles carefully. "Very well. I will return thanks." Effie prayed and thanked God for the provisions, and also asked that He would help the family in their time of need. When she finished her prayer, she noticed that everyone but Clarkie had a look of utter confusion on their faces. They were all wondering what she meant when she said "their time of need", but nobody wanted to be the one to ask. Effie instructed everyone to get a glass of lemon water from one of the three pitchers on the table. "It's hot today kids, we need to stay hydrated. Make sure to drink plenty of water, and Jacob, pour out that beer. That's the last one you're going to have today." Jacob pouted, but did as he was told.

The meal was delicious, and everyone ate heartily.   Conversation centered mostly on how work was going for everyone, Margo's pregnancy, and Jacob's latest adventures traveling the country.   When her guests had all eaten their fill, Effie clapped her hands to get everyone's attention.   "Clarkie and I are going to make coffee.   I want the rest of you to take folding chairs down by the lake and sit.   We're going to have a family meeting, and I will tell you why I've gathered you all together today."   Clarkie and Effie went to the camper to make the coffee while everyone else kept exchanging puzzled looks, all of them waiting to see who would speak first.   "I knew it," Sissy said, "I knew she had something up her sleeve."

The lake was beautiful, and a cool breeze blew in as the five sat waiting for Effie and Clarkie to bring the coffee. "Something's up and I don't like it," Sissy said as she crossed her legs, "Does anybody know what the hell is going on here?" "I don't know," Jacob sighed, "All I know is that mama insisted that we all be here this weekend. Maybe she's getting remarried or something." He was only half joking, but almost laughed out loud at the look the statement produced on Sissy's face. She looked as though she had just lifted the lid off of a trash can full of maggots. "I'm sure that everything is fine," Margo chirped, "And what if mama is getting remarried? I think that would be sweet." "You're a simpleton Margo, and you always have been!"

Sissy was shaking with anger. Surprisingly, this time it was Jeff who spoke up. "I think that we should all try to be civil and get along. We'll find out shortly what this is all about." A few silent moments later, Clarkie and Effie appeared with the carafes of coffee, poured a cup for everyone, and sat down. Effie took a sip of her coffee, savoring the smoky taste and smell of the roast that she had purchased especially for this day. Cheap, grocery store grind wouldn't give her the boost that she would need at this moment in time.

"Today I'm going to speak, and you're all going to listen. Not just hear me, but actually listen. When I am done saying all that I have to say, I will do my best to answer some of your questions, but let me warn you - you are all about to enter a chapter of your lives that is going to turn everything you believe upside down." Effie saw that she was actually scaring her children. "Fear of the truth is the darkness that has poisoned this family," she thought to herself, "It's time for us all to step into the light."

Chapter 4

"You children are all in the dark.   I'm sorry to be blunt, but facts are facts. The three of you grew up without a care in the world, sheltered completely by your father and myself.   Not a one of you knows who you really are, and that's our fault.   You don't know who your father was as a person, and you don't know me either.   How then could I possibly expect you to know yourselves?   We took the world that you were all destined to grow up in, and we changed it because we wanted to protect you.   Well now it's time to change it back.   It's time for you all to find out who we really are, and by extension, who you really are.   It's going to be scary, and it will be painful along the way too, but in the end I hope you all will have a freedom that you don't possess now."   Effie paused to sip her coffee and contemplate just how she was going to say what she needed to.   She almost wished that she had jotted down some notes to help her stay focused.

"You all knew your father as a successful hotel owner, and dedicated family man.   He was both of those, but there is so much more that you don't know, things he made me promise never to reveal.   He's dead now, and I realize that I have stunted each of you spiritually by allowing you to live with your heads in the sand.   I can no longer honor my promise to him as it will only continue to stunt any growth this family could have. You all know me as a virtuous woman, dedicated wife, and loving mother.   I am all of those things, but like your father, I have doors to my soul that have been closed and locked for many years.   Once these doors are open, they can never be closed again, and what's behind them is not going to be easy for you to deal with."

Effie closed her eyes for a moment, suddenly wishing she were somewhere else. She had honed indifference into a fine craft over the years, but that wasn't going to help her now. She had opened the floodgates and there would be no turning back. She knew her children had the strength to endure what was to come, but she also knew that they would have to lean on and support one another. She had serious doubts about their ability to "play well" together. When all was said and done, they would really have no other choice.

"When your father died, he left everything to me, knowing full well that when I pass I will leave it all to you. Two years ago, I gave you each $10,000 of your inheritance money. Sissy, I'm sure you squirreled yours away in an account somewhere. Margo, I know you used yours to pay for your wedding. Jacob, I imagine you pissed yours away and have nothing to show for it. None of that matters now. I'm giving the three of you a task to complete...together. Upon completion, I will be disbursing the remainder of your father's estate equally among the three of you." Sissy's eyes were wide now.

"I'm going away for a while, the only person who will know my whereabouts is Clarkie. The three of you will stay here at the lake. Jeff and Marcus, you will spend the night here tonight with your wives, but tomorrow you will go home. My three piglets will be here as a team. Have a discussion tonight, talk about who you think your father was, and who you think I am. In the morning, take those notions and throw them deep into the lake, they won't be able to comfort you any longer. You will then start your journey to find out who we really are, who YOU really are. The clues that you will need are all in the boxes in the camper. Clarkie will be staying at the house, so he is only fifteen minutes away if you should need anything, but none of you will be allowed to stay there.   Jacob, there is a tent in the back of Clarkie's jeep, I think you should use that and let the girls keep the camper."   At this point, Effie stopped talking for a moment to allow things to sink in, and also because she knew that there was bound to be some backlash. She had told the children that she would answer some of their questions.   Jacob and Margo were to stunned to think, let alone ask anything.   Still she waited patiently.   She didn't have to wait long, and naturally, it was Sissy who had something to say.

"Mother, this is ridiculous.   No, it's insane!   Are you suffering from dementia or something?   Do we need to call the doctor for you?   What the hell???" Sissy had tears in her eyes and Effie silently thought that this was the first time she had seen her shed a tear in many, many years.   Even when David died, Sissy's face was like a marble statue, without a hint of emotion, eyes as dry as the Sahara.   The other children were speechless, watching Sissy, allowing her to say what they were all thinking.

"Darlings, I am not nuts.   I love you all dearly, and none of this is to cause you any harm.   It will, mind you, be painful at times, but my prayer is that you will all rise out of the ashes like the Phoenix, healed and whole.   It's getting late and I have a flight to catch.   Clarkie will take me to the airport, and then return to stay with you for the night.   Your father and I have never kept secrets from Clarkie, he already has the blueprints to the new lives you are all about to build, but he won't give you the answers - only guidance along the way.   I cherish you all.   Pray for me as I will pray for you."

Effie quickly rose to her feet, and kissed each of them on the cheek before scuffling up the incline toward the jeep, fast enough that Clarkie had trouble keeping up with her.   As the jeep pulled out and made it's way down the dirt road, the five remaining souls sat in silence, stunned at the sudden turn the evening had taken.   Tears streamed down Sissy's face, the wall that she had built up for so many years suddenly seemed to have a crack in it.

Chapter 5

Dragonflies buzzed near the surface of the water.   A mourning dove cooed in the trees, pining for his mate.   A bass jumped, seizing his dinner.   Somewhere in the distance, children laughed and splashed in the lake.   These were the only sounds that broke the silence in the Banks camp.   Tears still streamed down Sissy's face, yet she uttered no sound. Jeff was visibly annoyed by the events of the day, Marcus sat nervously twitching his feet.   Margo and Jacob both looked at the ground, as if the answer to today's riddle would be found written in the grass somewhere.   Jacob fumbled in the pocket of his cargo shorts, producing a pack of cigarettes and a lighter. He lit one for himself, and then passed the pack to Sissy. The others watched in amazement as she took one out, lit it, and rolled her head back in ecstasy with the first drag. Sissy hadn't smoked in fifteen years, but this occasion seemed to call for a relapse.

Sissy wiped her eyes on the back of her arm and finally broke the silence. "I am a partner in a successful design firm. How does mother think that I have time to spend screwing around out here in the middle of nowhere? Jeff has his law firm, who is going to take care of everything in Chicago?" Jeff set his jaw. "Babe, that's the point of a partnership. Chris knew you'd be here for a couple of days anyway, he can handle the firm with the associates. We'll just tell him you need some more time. You haven't taken any time off since your father passed, and I don't remember the last time before that. I'm a big boy, I can manage to boss around the housekeeper and gardener just as well as you." He chuckled with that, and even Sissy seemed to crack half a smirk, if just for a moment. "I'll keep in touch with Clarkie so that you don't feel disconnected from everything. It's 1998, not 1968, we have the technology to communicate. I don't know what the hell your mother is up to, and if it was just about the inheritance I'd say screw it, but it seems like there is something deeper here that she wants the three of you to discover."

Sissy put her "I'm in charge" face on. "Okay, here's what were going to do. Jeff, you and Marcus go to the store for us.   We have leftovers for a few lunches and such, but we'll need things for breakfasts and snacks.   Get a few bags of ice and pick up two or three chest coolers.   Pick up a couple of cases of water, and a couple of cases of beer."

Margo's eyes widened. "Sissy, since when do you drink beer, and why two cases, isn't that a lot?" Sissy smirked, "I have a feeling that I'm going to be doing many things out of the norm this week. And yes, two cases is quite a bit, but don't forget we have 'numb nuts' with us." Jacob laughed heartily and loud, too amused by this sudden shift in the "Ice Queen" to be offended by her words. "I think that Clarkie expects us to be showing up to mom's house every day like little beggars, so let's be as self-sufficient here as we possibly can," Sissy paused, "and figure out as much as possible on our own without that smug old turd."

Jeff and Marcus kissed their wives, and then started off toward Jeff's overpriced "look at me" car.   It was now half past seven, and like most little upstate New York towns, the nearest small city with more than just a few "mom and pop" shops was at least twenty miles away. They would likely be gone for at least two hours.   Sissy was mentally exhausted, and she knew it was going to be a long night ahead of them.   "Jacob, I know you have plenty of beer left in that bucket of bolts of yours since mommy cut you off, why don't you liberate it, and bring one of the coolers down too."

Five minutes later, Jacob strolled down the incline, dragging a cooler full of half melted ice and beer. "Margo, there's some water and juice in there for you. I'm going to light a fire in the pit down here, and then we can get down to business." Jacob had always been the one who liked playing with fire as a child, and the girls exchanged smiles and giggles as they watched his face light up right along with the evening's camp fire. "Sissy, I'm going up by the camper to clean everything up so we don't have to worry about it later. You stay down here and babysit," Margo chuckled.

Jacob opened two beers, and handed one to his eldest sister. They sat looking at the lake, drinking their beer in silent thought. The heat of the day had dissipated a bit, replaced by a fresh breeze blowing in off of the lake. Sunset was at least an hour away, the perfect time for fishing. At the Banks camp, there would be a different kind of fishing going on tonight. Margo returned, face flushed, and sat down. "Apparently, there is a lot of things we don't know about mom and daddy," she said, "so lets talk about what we do know. Or I guess I should say, let's talk about what they've told us - what we THINK we know."

Chapter 6

The three siblings decided that they would get sleeping situations set up before they started a discussion that would likely last until sunrise. It was doubtful that they would get any actual sleep, but Jeff and Marcus would want to, and at any rate it seemed prudent to get the camp situated before anyone was too tired to do it. Jacob went to his car and grabbed the tent that Clarkie had leaned up against the trunk. He was happy to see that it was a good sized, four man tent, and not the army style pup tent that he'd imagined. The girls went to the camper and started making the two small beds.   It was a bit daunting to work around all of the boxes that Effie had left in there, and both girls wondered silently why they hadn't questioned the clutter when they had come in to use the bathroom before Effie's big announcement.   There had always been plenty of pillows and bed linens stored in the camper, but this time there was extra, no doubt purposely left by Effie for this occasion.   Jacob had decided to set up the tent down by the lake rather than close to the camper, so when the two girls finished, they took down blankets, sheets, and pillows for him.   After Jacob threw some more wood on the fire, the three resumed their places in their chairs overlooking the water.   They had all somehow missed the beauty of the sunset, each knowing they would have plenty of time to enjoy the beauty of the lake, since they had been sequestered here for the time being.   Not a one of them could know just how much they would need something beautiful to look at in the days to follow.

Jeff and Marcus returned at around ten with the provisions.   They found the three siblings joking and laughing about childhood foibles, Sissy and Jacob visibly buzzed.   "I guess they are procrastinating having any serious discussion for now," Marcus whispered.

"You two boys have a beer with us," Sissy slurred a bit, "And then take your asses up to bed in the camper. Margo and I are gonna hang out down here with the brat." "Don't you think you've had enough?" Jeff's face was pinched. "Cut her some slack, Jeff. When was the last time you saw her have any fun? God knows this may be our last night of actual fun for awhile," Jacob reasoned. "Alright, I guess," Jeff threw up his hands. The husbands shared a beer and a few laughs with the three, then kissed their wives and headed off to bed. Both men would have to catch a flight in the morning, Jeff back to Chicago, Marcus to the mountains of North Carolina to the Bed and Breakfast that he and Margo owned.

"Do you think mother is having a mid life crisis," Margo asked with her usual sweet sincerity. "Mid life?" Sissy was chortling. "She's 56. How the hell many 112 year old women do you know, honey?" Jacob couldn't hold back his booming laugh. "Sissy, by God, you should definitely drink more often!" They were all laughing now. "I've missed you guys. Why does it always take something bad to get us all in the same zip code?" Margo was starting to get sentimental now. Jacob put his arm around her. "We all went in different directions, Margo. It doesn't mean I don't love you both." "Amen," Sissy slurred a little too loudly and pointed the neck of her beer bottle toward the sky. They were all laughing again, Margo wishing that they could just laugh like this all night long, and then make the journey home in a day or two as originally planned.   "There's still hot coffee in one of the carafes," Jacob said, "I think Sissy and I should have some, and then we really need to put our heads together and hash out the story of mom and dad that we grew up with.   I'm sure not a one of us will remember all of the details, but between the three of us we can do it." Both girls nodded, Margo went for the carafe of coffee, and Jacob got up to throw more wood on the fire.

Marcus was still wide awake in the camper, while Jeff snored like a buzz saw. With the windows wide open, he couldn't hear exactly what was being said, but noticed that the laughter had stopped, and the voices had become more serious. He assumed that this meant the three were finally starting what they had been brought here to do.   "Dear God, please don't let my sweet Margo get hurt. Please give all three of them the strength and wisdom they will need to face whatever lies ahead."   He prayed for a few more moments before drifting off to a fitful sleep.   He was right to have prayed for sweet, mild, Margo.   In the days to come, she would find a strength within her that nobody suspected was there.

Chapter 7

Morning came too soon for the Banks clan, especially considering that the three siblings had been up until almost sunrise. Jeff had gotten up at six and gone for his usual run, Marcus opted to stay behind and sit on the dock with a cup of coffee. The two had decided to depart after breakfast, and after finding out what their wives and brother-in-law had come up with in the night's discussion. At eight, Marcus roused the three, who had all fallen asleep in the tent, Margo in the middle with the cushiest pillows and blankets, flanked on either side by Jacob and Sissy. "I'll make breakfast," Margo beamed, she was an incurable morning person.   Jacob and Sissy nodded and grunted, Jacob walking down to the water to wash his face and have a cigarette, Sissy off to the bushes for a good old fashioned dry heave.   The fire, which had almost gone out, had been resurrected by Marcus a half an hour before, and was perfect for cooking. "Thank you sweetheart," Margo winked noticing that her husband had already brought down all the pans, utensils, and food she would need to prepare the meal. She placed the grate across the fire, and put two oiled cast iron skillets on it to get hot.   Just twenty minutes later, the clan sat down to scrambled eggs, ham steaks, fried potatoes, and rye toast.   There was fresh fruit left over from the day before, and fresh coffee prepared by Marcus. About halfway through the meal, at which point Sissy began to look and feel more like herself, the siblings began to take turns speaking and piecing together the story of their parents as it had been relayed to them as children.

David Edward Banks was born in 1938 in Boston, MA. His father, Edward, was a real estate magnate, and chronic gambler. His mother, Ruth, had been a school teacher, but gave up working at Edward's insistence when they got married. When David was four years old, the family moved to Rochester, NY as Edward had acquired some hotel properties in the upstate region, and had grown tired of life in New England.

David was doted on by his mother, but received little attention from Edward. As Edward's fortune increased, so did his gambling, womanizing, and drinking. Young David both idolized and feared his father. When he was sixteen, Edward insisted that David learn the family business, and so he began traveling with Edward all over the country, looking for properties and hotels to acquire. David did not like talking about his childhood, so the siblings knew little else of it. Edward had died in 1980, at the age of 68, from lung cancer. Ruth was still living, and residing in Rochester.

Esther "Effie" Rachel Solomon was born in 1942 in Natchez, MS.   Her father Jacob worked as a janitor, her mother Rachel was a skilled seamstress who took in sewing and laundry while raising the children.   Both Effie's maternal, and paternal grandparents were Sephardic Jews who's families had emigrated to Natchez in the late 1700's when it was still controlled by the Spanish.   Effie's parents had converted to Christianity shortly after being married in the 1930's, and had consequently been almost completely cut off by both of their families. Although the conversion was mostly a political move to make their lives in the deep south easier, they joined the Presbyterian church and attended services every Sunday.   The household was a strict one, and Effie was expected to help with the raising of her four younger siblings.   Effie grew into a stunning young woman, and when she was caught having an illicit relationship with a local boy when she was 15, her parents threw her out of the house.   She moved to Savannah, GA to live with her sympathetic cousin Eliza who was 10 years older.   Once in Savannah, Effie dropped out of school and worked as a waitress to help her single cousin make ends meet.

In 1958, twenty year old David made a trip to historic Savannah to look at a hotel property that his father was interested in acquiring. He met 16 year old Effie while she was working at a diner, and it was love at first sight. David brought Effie home three months later, and in spite of his parents' disapproval, they were married in 1959. Clarissa was born in 1960, followed by Margo in 1963, and almost as an afterthought, Jacob in 1970. David and Effie had a close relationship in spite of the gambling addiction that he had inherited from his father. When David died suddenly of a heart attack in 1993, he had lost all but a quarter of his net worth to gambling. In spite of this, because he had been so successful, there was more than enough left to keep Effie comfortable, and provide a substantial inheritance to his children.

None of the children had any idea whether their maternal grandparents, Jacob and Rachel Solomon, were still living. Effie rarely spoke of them, and when she did, there was an overpowering sadness in her eyes. Consequently, she never spoke of her siblings either, it was as if she were an only child whose childhood stopped at the age of 15.

"That's quite a story in and of itself," Marcus noted. "What more could there possibly be?" Sissy shivered at the thought. "That's what we're all afraid of, I think. What could mama be keeping from us, considering all the dirt that she's already shared?" The group each poured another cup of coffee, and made their way up the incline to Jeff's car to say their goodbye. "We'll park Jeff's car at the airport for now and leave my minivan here for you guys to use. If one or both of us has a problem catching a flight out today, we'll get a hotel room for the night. We'll keep in touch either way," Marcus explained. "You two better take care of my sweetheart, and make sure she stays well hydrated. She still has three months left to bake that beautiful bun in there!" Jacob nodded. "Fancy pants Sissy has her cellular phone in case there's an emergency. The few people that live up here year round all have telephone service, so we know there's poles and lines up here. I'll have Clarkie look into getting us service this week." There were hugs all around, and then tears from the girls as they watched Jeff's shiny black car jog down the dirt road. Sissy wiped her eyes and resumed her self-appointed role as the boss. "I nominate Jacob to bring the first box out of the camper. Let's find out whatever the hell we're supposed to find out."

Chapter 8

After stepping into the camper, Jacob leaned up against the wall to let his eyes adjust to the lack of light compared to the bright sun outside. He was half entertaining the notion of drinking another beer and going back to bed for a while, but he knew the girls wouldn't stand for that. Once his eyes adjusted enough that he could see properly, he began surveying the boxes in front of him. "Surely, all of these can't be necessary," he thought, "she's sending us on a frigging scavenger hunt!" Looking at the boxes on top, he noticed that they had all been labeled in rather small, penciled handwriting. He opened the corner of a random box, and noticed that it was only about half full. Apparently, the boxes were meant more for organizational purposes than amount of storage. Three boxes stood out right away - they were marked "Clarissa", "Margo", and "Jacob". "I guess we'll start there," he said to himself, and stacked the three boxes together. Kicking the door open, he waddled down the two steps of the camper, and stepped one foot forward before falling squarely on his rump, dropping all three boxes. "So this is how today is going to go," he said aloud to himself.

Toddling the boxes down the incline was no easy feat, yet instead of helping, the girls sat at the foot of the dock giggling. "Thanks for the help, ladies!" Jacob couldn't help but smile, the levity in the air was something he figured they would all need today. Setting the boxes down in the grass at the foot of the dock, Jacob lit a cigarette. "These have our names on them. Shall we open them all at once, or have "Christmas in July" and take turns?" He didn't have to wait for an answer, as both girls began diving into their boxes. For the time being, he was content to watch them forage, and finish his cigarette. Both boxes contained pictures of the girls, report cards, small trinkets they had made as children in Sunday school, and a photocopy of their birth certificate.   Nothing stood out to either sister at this point.   "Jacob, open your box," Sissy ordered.

Jacob's box was a mirror image to the girls' at first glance, but at the bottom of the box was an index card.   It was the recipe for Effie's raisin cookies, not a copy, but the original that she had hand written before the children were born. Margo perked up, "I've been asking mom for that recipe for years!   Why would she put it in Jacob's box?"   She carefully read the recipe on the front of the card, then turned it over to reveal the baking details on the back.   Just below "yields three dozen cookies", Margo saw a penciled addition in Effie's handwriting. "Don't look for what you can see, look for what you can't see."   Margo was puzzled. "What does she mean by that?"

Sissy's analytical nature kicked in. "Let's spread out the contents of the boxes, put like objects together, and see if there are any differences."   They did so in about ten minutes time, and began scouring the various pictures and documents for differences.   Margo spoke up first.   "Sissy, your baby picture isn't dated the same as ours.   It has the actual day and month, but no year."

"Maybe it's because she was mom's first," Jacob reasoned, "and also mom was a teen mother, probably unsure of herself at that point."   "That doesn't sit right with me," Sissy scowled.   Another picture of Effie, herself as a newborn, and a woman she'd never seen caught Sissy's eye.

"That must be mother's cousin Eliza," Margo reasoned.   "Yeah, but I wasn't born in Georgia, Margo, I was born here. This picture was clearly taken in Georgia, we don't have gardenia bushes here. Nobody would take a brand new baby on a trip that long in those days."   Sissy began to feel sick.   She scurried off to the bushes, Margo just steps behind. Margo was always the mother figure.

"Um….." they heard Jacob say on their way back to the dock. "Sissy, I've been wondering why mother put photocopies of our birth certificates in here. I've had my original since I left home and I thought you two did also. I've noticed something on these photocopies though. On mine and Margo's, you can clearly see where the original had an official seal from Monroe county, NY. Yours doesn't have that! In the copy you can see the spot where the seal would be has been torn off. Didn't you ever notice that when you had to use your birth certificate for your driver's license, or college, or marriage license?" "No! Daddy always came with me and produced whatever documents I needed. I asked him once when I was sixteen to see my birth certificate and he brushed me off. My God," Sissy exclaimed, "What is mother hiding about my birth?" Margo hugged her tightly. "We'll get to the bottom of all of this."

There was a rumble in the distance, and then with a cloud of dust, Clarkie's car pulled onto the grass at the top of the camp. Upon seeing the girls embracing one another, and the disconcerting look on Jacob's face, he knew that they must have found a piece of Effie's puzzle. He wiped the sweat off his brow with a handkerchief, and made his way down the incline.   The girls separated, stood back, and Sissy suddenly looked like a ravenous wolf.   "Sam Clark, where is my original birth certificate?   I want to see it, and I want to see it now!"   Clarkie had come prepared, and pulled a long, slim envelope out of his back pocket.   "This is all I can show you, Clarissa."

Chapter 9

Hands trembling, Sissy opened the envelope that Clarkie had produced. Although it seemed more official, on thick, textured, pale yellow paper, it was the same document that had been photocopied and put in Sissy's box. The corner where an official seal would go had been carefully torn off. "What the hell, Sam? This is the same birth certificate that mother put in my box. This explains nothing!" Clarkie shifted his weight, back aching from having slept on Effie's couch last night. "I know dear. That's because the original is still in Chatham county, Georgia....where you were born.   Your mother and father had a certified copy here, but your mother took it with her.   It seems that she wants you to track down the original."   "So this one's a fake?"   Sissy was red faced. "I'm afraid it is, Clarissa."   He went to pat her arm, but she pulled away.   "Why would they tear the corner off of this document?"   Sam scratched his head, "I'm guessing your mother thought it might be easier to explain a torn document than one that was intact but obviously missing something."   Sissy was indignant,   "I need to talk to mother's cousin.   How the hell do I find her? I don't know her, and she doesn't know me.   For all I know, she may even be dead!"   Clarkie smirked, "Actually

Clarissa, she's expecting your call.
Come back to the house with me."

The three siblings agreed that Sissy
would go back to the house, while Jacob
and Margo continued to empty out the
boxes.   "I'm leaving my cellular phone
here if you guys need it, I'll try to be back
by supper time.   Maybe I'll bring us back
a pizza from town."   Jacob looked
concerned.   "Sissy, no matter what you
find out today, remember, all three of this
are in this together.   I know we don't
always see eye to eye, but I love you."
Oldest and youngest embraced before

Sissy got into the passenger seat of Clarkie's car.

The drive from the lake to Effie's house was beautiful. They passed by farm after farm on the dirt road, taking in the scenery. Deer grazed in the open fields, rabbits and squirrels ran across the road, and folks enjoying the sunshine on their porches waved as if they were old friends. When they turned left onto the paved road toward Effie's house, Sissy began to breathe heavily, anxiety taking it's toll on her. She pulled a bottle out of her purse, took a single pill from it, and swallowed it without bothering to get a sip of water to wash it down.   Sissy had suffered from anxiety for as long as she could recall, and now began to wonder if it had something to do with the fact that life as she had known it was a total farce. Memories came over her like a tidal wave as they pulled up the long driveway to Effie's large, two story colonial home. Clarkie parked in front of the three car garage instead of in it.   "I'm going to sit here for just a minute, Sam.   You go ahead on in."   He nodded and made his way into the house.

Several minutes passed before Sissy found herself in the foyer of her childhood home.   This was initially the family's summer home, the main house being in Rochester close to the one owned by her paternal grandparents, but when she was about ten years old, her father had sold the main house and moved here permanently.   Nobody ever gave her or Margo an explanation for the move, it just was what it was.   Shortly after, Jacob was born.   Sissy remembered her grandparents coming to see the new baby, and then an intense argument with a plethora of angry words exchanged. After that, the children only saw David's parents at their home in Rochester, and Effie never went along with them.

Sissy made her way to the breakfast room off of the kitchen, the most comfortable place she could think of to use the phone. It was always such a cheerful room, full of light, with plenty of lush houseplants and a collection of Effie's fresh potted herbs. With shaky hands, she pulled the paper that Clarkie had given her in the car out of her purse, and dialed the number. After three rings, she heard a voice on the other end of the line say "Hello?" Sissy swallowed hard, "Hello, is this Ms. Solomon? Ms. Eliza Solomon?" A short pause. "Clarissa, is that you honey?" The voice was soft and sweet, with a gentle southern drawl. "Yes ma'am, but I….I don't know what to say." Sitting in her kitchen in Georgia, Eliza could only imagine the anxiety that was washing over Sissy.   She decided to spare her young cousin the burden of asking all the difficult questions.

"Clarissa, honey, listen to me.   I know y'all are going through a tough time there, lots of changes, lots of questions.   Fix yourself a cup of tea, I'll wait here on the line, and I'll give you the answers you called for."

Sissy took Eliza up on her offer.   She made herself a cup of tea, and went to the top of the spice cupboard to find the pack of cigarettes and ashtray that Effie always hid there and thought nobody knew about.   She sat at the table, lit a cigarette, and put the phone to her ear. "Ms. Solomon, are you still there?"   A small sigh, "Yes sugar, I'm here.   Call me Liza, everyone does.   Now all I want you to do is sit tight and listen.   I'll tell you about your mother, about how you happened to be born here in Georgia."

Chapter 10

It all seemed like a dream, a very strange, and not so comfortable dream. As Sissy sat listening to Liza on the phone, she kept waiting, hoping, imagining she'd wake up in the tent next to Margo.   Surely, this dream was brought on by all of the rich food, the heat of the day, and too many beers.   She could accept the fact that Effie had cracked a bit, and sent her children on this bizarre sort of scavenger hunt, but she could not accept what she was hearing now.   There was no way that this girl she was hearing about was her mother.   It couldn't be the same Effie, the devoted wife and mother who sat in church every Sunday. Sissy hung up the phone, hands still trembling, and lit a cigarette. She looked at her watch and noted that it was now six o'clock. She had been on the phone with Liza for several hours and hadn't even realized it. Clarkie, who had been listening from the kitchen, called out to her. "Clarissa, is everything okay?" She snorted, "Really? What do you think, genius?" She suddenly realized that this whole time, she had been targeting Clarkie, when really it was her mother that she was upset with. "I'm sorry Sam. Could you come in here please?" Clarkie made his way to the breakfast room, not really sure what to expect from Sissy. "I need to sit on the porch and try to put this all together in my head for a bit.   I need to try to process what I've just been told, if there's any way to really do that.   Would you mind trying to call Jeff and Marcus, find out if they've made it home?"

Clarkie smiled, "Of course, Clarissa.   By the way, your mother has three bottles of white wine in the refrigerator if you need it. She says it's for cooking, but…"   he winked, and they both laughed.

On the porch with her glass of wine in hand, Sissy began to take what Liza had told her and weave it all together.

Liza's father Abram was one of the few family members that had not cut ties with Effie's parents after their conversion. Abram was a successful jeweler in Savannah, and would often send money, what he called "gifts", to Effie's parents in Natchez.   When Liza was ten, Effie was born, and Liza accompanied her parents to Natchez to see the new baby.   Liza was utterly infatuated with her baby cousin, and began a lifelong habit of writing to her from Savannah every day. The two would rarely get to see one another due to the distance that separated them, but they formed a loving friendship through their letters and postcards.   Liza was an avid cook, and when she turned eighteen and had no suitors waiting in the wings, Abram purchased a small diner for her to run, with an attached apartment upstairs. Effie and Liza would dream together about the two of them someday expanding this business together, neither having any thoughts of love, marriage, or family.   All of that would change in a sudden and appalling way.

When Effie was fifteen, she was caught having relations with an older boy by one of her brothers.   Her father Jacob was livid, announcing that she must leave the house at once, never to return.   Effie's mother pleaded with her husband, who agreed to allow Effie to stay in the house just long enough to make arrangements for her to go elsewhere. A telephone call was placed to Liza, and the next morning Effie was on a train bound for Savannah. Liza promised that she would make sure Effie finished school, and would provide her with an after school job waiting tables, so that she could save money for her future.

Once in Savannah, Effie felt free from the strict rules an ideals that she had been raised with. She fell in love with the spirit of the city, a melting pot of many cultures.   The ancient live oaks draped in their coats of Spanish moss reminded her of her home in Natchez, but their was a buzz about Savannah, almost like she could hear jazz wherever she went and she felt a certain electricity in the air. She took to wearing a gardenia in her hair, fresh from the abundance of gardenia bushes around the city.   She adored the historic squares and cobblestone streets, and could get lost for hours at the markets on the waterfront.   After about a week, she dropped out of school, reasoning with Liza that it wouldn't be necessary for her to finish, since the cousins were going to grow a business together, and besides, it was almost summer.   Effie was quite a beauty, with her dark alluring eyes, espresso hued loose curls, rich olive skin, and voluptuous breasts.   She became quite popular with the men folk in town, and her tips were always plentiful.   She would flounce around the diner, singing popular standards of the day, and flirt shamelessly.   In spite of her popularity at the diner, Effie grew bored, anxiously awaiting the next adventure that life would offer her.   She needn't wait long.

One afternoon, Effie had a strange patron at one of her tables.   She was a tall woman, probably in her mid fifties, with platinum blonde hair, heavy makeup, and covered in colorful jewelry. She introduced herself to Effie as Madame LeBlanc. Effie found herself immediately fascinated with this strange new character. "I've had my eye on you, and you've got lots of tongues wagging in our quaint little city. Princess, how would you like to work for me, hmm?" Effie was puzzled by the question, and strangely excited. "Doing what ma'am? I already work here, waiting tables." Madame LeBlanc laughed, cigarette smoke streaming from her nostrils, "Darling, when I show you how easily you can make money and friends in this town, you'll never serve another greasy burger again!" She went on to explain that Effie would "entertain" gentlemen. She would accompany them to dinners, nightclubs, and be a companion to them while they were in town on business.   Naive Effie thought this sounded like a dream come true.   Madame LeBlanc smirked, "Meet me tonight at this address, and not a word to your precious cousin, no?"   She handed Effie a wad of cash, and a card with an address on it.   "Fix yourself up darling, no kiddie stuff.   You're a woman, not a girl."

That night, while Liza dozed in their living room with a novel, Effie sneaked out and made her way to the address on the card.   The old Georgian mansion was a hotbed of activity!   Beautiful girls talked and danced with mostly older, but distinguished looking gentlemen.   "This is Mr. Brown.   You will accompany him upstairs for a chat and get to know one another," Madame LeBlanc made a sweeping gesture toward the enormous winding staircase.   Within an hours time, Effie learned what she had suddenly become - a high priced call girl.   She was mortified at first, but also strangely exhilarated.   Any reservations that she harbored evaporated when Madame LeBlanc handed her a large sum of cash. "I take thirty percent, but this is still more than you make in a week at that shitty diner, no?"   Effie had made a life altering decision that night, one that would haunt her and those she loved for years to come.

Effie began sneaking out every night after that. Liza had seen her slip out once or twice, and thought maybe she had a new suitor. She didn't want to be strict on her young cousin, but when she noticed a significant change in Effie, she became concerned. Effie's work ethic at the diner had slipped, she was constantly tired, and had little interest in spending time with Liza. One night, Liza pretended to fall asleep on the couch with a book. Through squinted eyelids she watched her young cousin put on clothes that easily could have cost her two weeks worth of tips from the diner, paint her face, douse herself in perfume, and slip out the door.   Liza decided she needed to follow her.

Effie walked the back streets and alleys as much as possible, so as not to draw attention to herself.   Liza quietly stayed several feet behind, hiding behind parked cars and trash cans whenever possible. Effie finally made her way to the large hotel on Broughton Street and went inside.   Liza watched through the windows as she met an older gentleman at the bar, and the two sat down to order food and drinks.   "What is she doing with a man old enough to be her father," Liza wondered.   Two hours later, dinner and drinks having been finished, the couple made their way out of the hotel and into the street.   Liza prayed that they would be walking to wherever they were headed next, and the odds were in her favor. She was able to follow the couple block after block until they reached Madame LeBlanc's mansion.   From the hedges outside, Liza watched as the gentleman handed Madame LeBlanc an envelope, and the pair made their way up the stairs. Madame LeBlanc opened the envelope, examined the sum of cash inside, and seemingly satisfied, stuffed it in her clutch.

Liza, who was not ignorant to what was going on inside, had seen enough for one night.   Heartbroken and sick, she made her way home.

Just before dawn, Effie crept into the apartment, still a little inebriated, and exhausted.   She made her way to her bedroom where, unbeknownst to her, Liza sat on the bed waiting.   "Tell me it's not true Effie, tell me that my fifteen year old cousin is not a prostitute."   "Liza, I…."   Effie hung her head, she wasn't really ashamed of herself, but she hated the disappointment on Liza's face.   "I'm not a prostitute, I'm an escort. I make men happy, and they pay me handsomely for it." The two cousins embraced for what seemed like an eternity, not a word spoken between them. Liza weighed her options carefully. She was filled with emotions of shock, disgust, shame, fear, and guilt, and she dared not act on any one of them without pause. She reasoned that this was partly her fault, after all, she had promised to keep Effie in school, promised to keep a watchful eye on her, promised to keep her safe. "We'll talk in the morning Effie. I'll put a note on the door of the diner and we'll open it two hours late. Get some sleep."

The next morning, over coffee, the cousins talked. Effie was adamant that although this was not a lifelong career choice, she was not about to give it up now. Liza was stuck. She couldn't throw her young cousin out! Effie would probably find somewhere to stay among those who would exploit her, but would she be safe? What would the repercussions be if the family found out what was happening here? What would happen to the diner if the locals found out what Effie was up to? The cousins came to an agreement. Effie would no longer walk the Savannah streets at night, she would take a cab to wherever she needed to meet someone. She would give up her job at the diner, pay rent to help Liza make ends meet, and agree to stop working for Madame LeBlanc within the year.   The two cousins would then take the money Effie was saving, and expand the business, maybe even open another diner across town.   Liza wasn't completely at ease with this arrangement, but was hopeful that if she could just hold on, things would get better.   Liza was concerned about Effie getting pregnant. Effie explained, "Madame LeBlanc has shown us that there are many ways you can please a gentleman without having actual intercourse.   Most of the time, it works.   She's told us that when we can't avoid intercourse, we are to try to pull away before they….you know.   On the rare occasion that a pregnancy occurs, Madame LeBlanc has the girl go away for a couple of days to "take care of it", but she's never happy about it.   Fewer girls attract less business, I guess."

Life for the cousins seemed placid for a time.   Liza tried not to think about what Effie was doing, and now that there were no secrets between them, their close bond and friendship resumed.   Effie poured a fair amount of her earnings into making improvements in the diner.   An expansion was added, allowing for more tables, and Liza was able to hire a cook and additional waitresses.   Effie seemed determined to keep her promise that she would give up working for Madame

LeBlanc by the end of the following summer.

In the spring of 1958, Effie's life would take another sudden, and very sharp turn. Underground gambling was taking off in the cities of the deep south, and Madame LeBlanc was not about to let opportunity pass her by. The cellar of the old mansion, which had served as the kitchen and wine cellar when the home was built, had initially been turned into a pub of sorts by the Madame. In a mere two days time, it had been filled with card tables, a roulette wheel, craps tables, and had been staffed with men in tuxedos to keep the money flowing.   The girls were encouraged to utilize any time they weren't entertaining a client upstairs by serving drinks and making conversation with the gambling clientele.

One rainy night that March, Effie made her way downstairs and her heart stopped.   At one of the card tables sat a duo of gentlemen, obviously by their looks, father and son.   The younger of the two had strawberry blonde hair, ice blue eyes, fine chiseled features, and a smile like none other Effie had ever seen.

Practically pushing the other girls out of her way, she made her way to their table, introduced herself, and offered them drinks.   The young man seemed as smitten with Effie as she was with him. He told her his name was David, he was born in Boston, now lived in Rochester, and he was here celebrating his twentieth birthday with his father while also on business in Savannah.   David's father excused himself, and twenty minutes later, Madame Leblanc summoned Effie upstairs.   "You have been selected as a birthday gift darling.   You will be spending the night upstairs with that luscious young man you've been talking to, his father paid very handsomely.   You do whatever he wants, but don't be daft!

I saw how you looked at him. Men like him do not fall in love with girls like you!"

It obviously wasn't the first time Effie had ever had sex, but it was the first time she had ever been made love to, the first time she experienced her body's reaction to a true lover. There was something safe and familiar about David, almost as though their souls had met before. He touched her tenderly, lovingly, not pawing at her like all the other men. When he saw Effie, he saw a beautiful woman, the woman of his dreams, and it showed in his eyes, in his touch. He didn't see

Effie as a prostitute, he let himself dream that she was his bride and this was their wedding night.   When they had finished their love making, he held her, kissing her neck, stroking her hair, and they talked late into the night.   Effie prayed that she would see him again, allowed herself to believe that they were star crossed lovers destined to be together forever.   They left one another in the morning, David promising that he would see her again. In the few hours that they had shared together, both Effie and David had fallen madly, deeply in love.

Over the next two months, David kept finding "business reasons" to return to Georgia. He and his father Edward were indeed looking at properties in the area, but Edward knew why David really continued to go back. He dismissed it as a youthful fling, nothing more. Since their first meeting early that spring, Effie had stopped letting customers have intercourse with her. She would pleasure them in other ways, but in her eyes the very essence of her belonged to David. When the young couple began exchanging letters regularly, Edward was concerned. "She's a whore, David, nothing more. Don't get me wrong, she's gorgeous, and one day I may even pay for some time with her, but you're going to have to stop this eventually.

You need to marry soon, a lady of your own class.   It will kill your mother if she finds out about any of this."   David was undeterred.   He rented a large apartment on the waterfront for Effie, and promised to visit her weekly.   Effie walked away completely from her business arrangement with Madame LeBlanc, who was furious, and went back to helping Liza with the diner.

In August, Effie found out she was pregnant.   She was terrified, but took solace in the fact that her menses had stopped in May, and David was the only man she had had intercourse with since March.   She knew that he was the only man that could be the father.   David was over the moon.   For months they made every effort to keep Effie's condition from his father, until one fateful day in January of 1959.   Edward had come to town to check up on his young son, noting that his excursions to Savannah had been become more frequent, and that his time spent there had grown longer.   Arriving at the return address he had seen so many times on Effie's letters to David, he was allowed entry by a housekeeper, only to find a heavily pregnant Effie on the arm of his son.   "This will need damage control," he thought, and began hatching a plan.

Edward was pensive. "The two of you will get married at city hall, immediately. It appears that you're really in love, but at this point, I don't care. David will remain here to "take care of my southern business dealings", and that will take a long time, at least, that's the story that we'll divulge. I'll tell everyone that you've fallen for a local girl, and that with my blessing, you eloped to spare the girl's family the expense of a lavish wedding. You will provide me all of the details of the child's birth, and at the beginning of the new year, I will pay whatever necessary to have a birth certificate made that states that the child was born in Rochester in 1960. None of our family or friends will see the certificate, and in turn we will tell them that your baby was born here, but again in 1960.   I won't have a bastard for a grandchild. When the child is about three years old, the two of you will return to Rochester. By that time, having not laid eyes on you for so long, nobody will think to question the baby's age, and will probably just assume that he or she is highly developed, because you yourself are so damned smart!"   With that he shot a disdainful look at David, who noted the sarcasm.   The very next day, at two o'clock in the afternoon, the couple were officially married at city hall.

Clarissa Eliza Banks was born March 17, 1959. According to Liza, she was a beautiful, happy baby, and the apple of her father's eye. The couple carried out Edward's plan, enjoying three years in Savannah with their new addition. In July of 1962, they returned to Rochester as planned. Edward had been right, nobody thought to question the baby's age, as Sissy had been a small infant to begin with. David and Effie had agreed that neither of them would ever reveal to her the truth of her conception. She needn't ever know that she was conceived out of wedlock by a teenage prostitute.

Sissy finished her glass of wine and poured another.   It had been an emotionally draining evening, and she wasn't necessarily looking forward to hashing out all of the details with her siblings.   She would go back inside soon, find out if Jeff was home, think about picking up some dinner to take back to the lake.   "We need to find out what else mother has been hiding, but for now," she thought, "I just need to sit still."

Chapter 11

It was the longest telephone conversation that Sissy and Jeff had had since they were courting. She couldn't help but remember how back then, they would often fall asleep on the phone with one another. "Are you okay, Clare?" It was also the first time in a long time that she could remember Jeff using his nickname for her. "I'm fine Jeff. I mean, I will be fine. It's just a lot to process. I'm not looking forward to whatever else she has waiting for us to discover." Jeff sighed, "I know she said that you guys were supposed to do this on your own, but do you want me to put some things on hold and come back out there? I'm worried about you!" Sissy felt a pang of longing for Jeff, something she hadn't experienced since their marriage had started to get rocky. In the past two years, her addiction to work, several failed attempts to conceive, and his indifference toward marital counseling had all taken a heavy toll. "I love you Jeff. I'm so sorry for not always showing you that. I want us to get back to the old us when I come home, if that's what you want." Jeff was choked up, another rarity for him. "Yes Clare, I do. I love you! Please call me as soon as you can." Tears flowing freely, Sissy hung up the phone. After composing herself, she called Marcus to tell him that they were all fine and that Margo would call soon.   Clarkie had told her, before she had made the calls to Jeff and Marcus, that telephone service would be installed at the lake the next morning.   "How did you manage that so fast," she had asked. "You know that I have connections everywhere," he had responded with a hearty laugh and a wink.

It was nearing eight o'clock and Sissy was eager to get back to the lake.   As much as she hated this quest that they were all on, she couldn't help but be curious about what Margo and Jacob had found in Effie's assortment of boxes.

She put the half empty bottle of wine back in the fridge, and put a full bottle, wine glass, and corkscrew in a paper bag to take with her. She called out to Clarkie, who was almost immediately in the kitchen, as if no matter where she had been in the house that day, he was just around the corner. "Clarkie, lets blow this joint! I want to stop at Tony's Pizzaria in town and pick up a pie." He smiled at the usually stuffy Clarissa suddenly using slang like a "normal" person. "Yes, ma'am!"

After picking up their dinner, Sissy had Clarkie stop at the local mini mart, where she purchased a bag of marshmallows to roast on the fire, and a carton of cigarettes. She was usually very health conscious, but that had all gone out the window for now. She giggled to herself when the clerk asked for identification for the smokes. She had always looked young for her age, but couldn't help but find amusement in the irony that she was actually a year older than the date on her license. The drive back to the lake seemed different now, almost as if knowing the truth had opened her eyes for the first time. The colors seemed richer, images sharper somehow. "Clarkie, I know that you knew about this, have always known about this. You must also know all about whatever else mother has stuffed away for us to find. How do you live with it, with the secrets I mean?" He smirked a little, "I take lots of antacids, and a healthy dose of valium." The pair laughed heartily and long. Sissy felt as though she had just learned how to laugh in the last two days. Oddly, the "dirty" details of her parents' meeting and her conception had set her free. As they pulled into the lake lot, they could see that there was still a nice fire going on the lower part of the lot. Jacob and Margo were on the dock playing cards and laughing like children. Sissy smiled. "Sam, do you want to stay and eat with us? We'll have plenty, there's no way we'll eat two large pizzas." "No, thank you young lady. Enjoy your night with your comrades.   Call me tomorrow once the phone's set up."   Sissy hugged Clarkie's neck and kissed his cheek, something she hadn't done since she was a little girl. As he pulled away, a single tear ran down his cheek.

"Sissy!"   Margo struggled to get up, and waddled over to hug her sister.   Jacob was right behind, and all three embraced. "Listen guys, I'll tell you the whole story, but first we're going to eat pizza and play cards!"   Jacob had pulled four Adirondack chairs and a wooden coffee table out of the overstuffed shed behind the camper, and set them up on the end of the dock.   The dock was shaped like a "T", with the end platform being fatter, making it a patio of sorts.   He had lit four gas lanterns to provide them some light, and a couple of citronella candles to keep the bugs at bay.   "Who's the fourth chair for," Margo asked.   "I dunno," Jacob swatted at a mosquito, "I thought maybe Clarkie would hang out.   He's usually around whenever there's food."   Sissy laughed, "You're an ass bro, but I love you."   Jacob reeled a bit, he couldn't remember the last time he had received any genuine affection from his eldest sister, or the last time she had called him "bro".   "Let's play "war", it's a fun game and doesn't require a whole lot of concentration," Jacob reasoned.

Tony's pizza was just as the three had remembered.   The crust was crispy on the outside, soft on the inside, covered with a rich homemade sauce that was heavy with garlic and basil, and an abundance of cheese that was slightly browned on the top.   There was a levity in the air reminiscent of their childhood here on the lake, and they laughed and swapped memories as they ate.   After his first piece of pizza, Jacob had taken the liberty of bringing the big chest cooler full of ice, bottled water, and beer out to the dock.   Sissy poured herself a glass of the wine she'd smuggled from Effie's, re-corked the bottle, and put it in the cooler.   Once full, they sat for awhile, letting their pizza settle.   "This is fun guys!   Can you believe we're actually having fun?" Margo was beaming. Jacob and Sissy exchanged a "she's such a dork" look, and laughed.

The moon was bright and large over the placid lake. Sissy was a little bit tipsy as she exclaimed, "Hey! You know what's fun? Moonlight swimming! Let's go swimming!" Jacob sarcastically commented, "Mother always said we had to wait until an hour after we eat to go swimming." "She also said we shouldn't have sex until we were married and we should always tell the truth," Sissy retorted, wishing she could pull the words back inside her mouth the moment they flew out.   Jacob and Margo were wide eyed.   "Don't mind me guys, we'll talk later.   For now, we swim!"   Margo looked puzzled, "I don't think I brought a bathing suit and anything else that would be okay to swim in is in the camper." Sissy chortled, "That's never stopped us before!"   She stripped to her bra and underpants and jumped in, enjoying the rush of the cool water on her skin. Margo blushed and followed suit, Jacob joining in his boxer shorts.   They laughed and splashed each other like children, and for this brief moment, all was well in the world again.

Chapter 12

Sissy had awoken at six o'clock feeling better than she had remembered in a long time. Considering the mixture of wine, greasy pizza, roasted marshmallows, and staying up way too late, she had thought that she would not wake up feeling very well. This morning, however, she felt more alive, less restricted, as if a weight had been lifted off of her chest. Leaving her siblings to their slumber, she got up, made coffee with the old fashioned percolator on the campfire, and made her way to the end of the dock for a cigarette. "Coffee always tastes better outdoors," she thought to herself.   After their swim, a lot of laughs, and some more card games the night before, the siblings all agreed that they were worn out, and Sissy could tell them all about her phone conversation with Liza in the morning.   Somehow, they had all ended up sleeping in the tent again instead of the girls utilizing the camper. Though they didn't speak about it, they all had a sense of safety and security sleeping in the tent together.   "It's us against the world now," Sissy thought to herself.   The practical part of her brain told her that this train of thought might be over-exaggerated, but she had started to rely more on the emotional part of her brain.   Sissy had decided that in order to deal with what she had just learned about her parents and herself, she would have

to put her heart above her head,
otherwise she would probably go mad.

An hour and a half later, Jacob made his
way out of the tent.   Sissy was at the fire,
making fresh coffee.   She had heard him
pass gas a couple of times in the tent,
and had assumed that meant he would
be making his appearance soon.
"Mornin' Siss," he mumbled, and made
his way to the bushes to relieve himself.
Sissy laughed at the irony of the three of
them here at the lake acting like
teenagers, in light of the fact that she had
just found out she was closer to forty than

everyone thought. "Hey butthead," she hollered toward the bushes, "when you're done over there, go wake up your other sister. The guys should be here soon to put the new phone line in, and you know how embarrassed she'll be if she has to come out at the last minute with her hair all messy and her breath smelling like a cat's ass!" Jacob laughed his usual booming laugh, he liked this newer version of Sissy, the version that drank, and joked, and LIVED. Once everyone was awake, the three reconvened on the dock with their coffees, enjoying the morning sun and the cool breeze coming off of the lake. At eight o'clock on the dot, the men from the phone company showed up, no doubt Clarkie had paid someone generously for service to be installed so quickly.   Jacob went up and granted the men entrance to the camper and shed, then returned with the pot of coffee to the dock.

Sissy knew her time had come, and the words began pouring out of her like water from a broken dam.   She spared no details of what she had been told by Liza on the telephone, and her story was as animated as any Hollywood blockbuster. She sobbed, she yelled, she wrung her hands as if squeezing the dirty details out of her own skin, and when she finished her face looked like it had been lit on fire, and then the fire had been beaten out with a rake. "My God," was all Margo could muster, and Jacob's face had gone completely ashen. All three of them were glad that they had skipped breakfast, it wouldn't have been a pretty sight for anyone to see them each vomit into the lake. They sat in silence for what seemed like an eternity, Jacob and Margo trying to make sense of what they'd just heard, Sissy trying to compose herself. Finally, Sissy decided it would be her job to break up the negative energy she had released on everyone. With a twinkle in her eye, she got up, pretended she was going for more coffee, and tipped Jacob's chair forward, spilling him off the end of the dock. Poor Margo, pregnant and having had too much coffee, immediately wet her pants. "Dammit Sissy, I have a pack of smokes and a lighter in my pocket!" Jacob was red faced and furious, which only made the incident more amusing to the girls. Noticing eventually that Margo had wet herself, Jacob loosened up and joined in on the laughter. "The telephone guys probably think we're drunk," Sissy fought to get the words out, her laughter leaving her short of breath. "It's not a bad idea," Jacob retorted. Margo got up, went to the ladder, and lowered herself into the water. She and Jacob floated on their backs and kicked their legs, trying to splash Sissy on the dock. For a brief moment, the "old" Sissy made an appearance. "Um, guys, we do have some things to get done today." "Yeah," Margo shot back, "and

I'm not about to do it with pissy pants!"
Laughter exploded in the camp again as
Sissy yelled "Cannonball," jumping in
directly between her brother and sister,
dousing them with her splash.   She had,
at least, remembered to empty her
pockets first, a luxury that Jacob hadn't
had.

The men from the telephone company
hollered down that they were finished, so
Jacob got out of the water and headed up
to get all the details about their new
service.   The girls floated on their backs
in the water, Margo looking like a small

island with her pregnant belly protruding above the surface of the water. "Sissy, I just have to ask, do you believe everything mother's cousin told you is true?" "Why would she lie? After all, mom obviously wanted me to make contact with her, and Clarkie was in on the whole thing." Margo sighed, "True enough. It's just hard to believe that our mother was a….well, you know." "I know, trust me, I know," Sissy motioned toward Jacob, "I'm worried about that one there. You know how close he is to mom and how he idolizes her. What kind of other crazy, messed up things are we going to find out? I don't think he can handle much more."

Chapter 13

Sissy and Margo sat by the fire having a cup of coffee.   After the impromptu morning swim, they had changed their clothes and hung the wet stuff on the clothesline.   Sissy was putting a braid in her hair when Jacob came down announcing, "The phone is in!   The new phone number is written next to it on the counter.   I'm going to change out of my wet clothes."   Jacob disappeared into the tent to change, Margo waddled up to the camper to place a call to Marcus, while Sissy sat finishing the braid in her long, wet hair.

"Jacob, what did you and Margo find yesterday while I was gone?" Jacob exited the tent, dressed for the day, put his hair in a ponytail, and threw his wet clothes on the grass. "We found some weird stuff, Siss. An odd collection of receipts, property deeds, seemingly unrelated papers all together in a garbage bag, and family pictures with faces cut out." He scratched his head. "We went through every single box in there, consolidated them, and only kept out the things that don't make any sense to us. We put the stuff that we don't think is relevant in the shed up by the camper, and moved the stuff that seems fishy to the shed down here. I figure we should go through it when Margo gets off of the phone." "Sounds like a plan," Sissy lit a cigarette, "but what kinds of things don't make sense?"   Jacob sighed.   "I think we've taken a lot of things for granted Siss, never thought long and hard about things.   I guess we've never had a reason to until mom dropped all of this in our laps."   Sissy nodded in agreement, "You're probably right there.   I'm not making excuses for her, but I'm guessing that wherever mom is, she feels just as confused and crappy about all of this as we do."   She was feeling Jacob out to see how much strain had been put on his relationship with Effie, and his reaction confirmed what she had suspected since bringing it up to Margo last night.   He gave a slight eye roll, and grabbed a beer out of the cooler.   "Jacob, I know you're hurting, and I'm not trying to minimize that, but it's not even noon yet. Please don't get completely blotto today, okay?" He didn't even look at her as he said, "Yup," and drank half the bottle of beer in one chug.

Margo rejoined the gang, happy and bright after her telephone conversation with Marcus. She chattered on for a minute or two about how things were going at home, how Marcus had booked a celebrity to stay at the Bed and Breakfast next month, wondering out loud what foods she should prepare for the event. Jacob couldn't help but smile at his sweet sister, she never seemed to have a bad day. "Haven't you had celebrities before, Margo?" He had reasoned that he shouldn't let his mood dampen her excitement, but couldn't help but think that there were more pressing issues at hand than who stayed at the Bed and Breakfast. She seemed to understand, and decided to drop the conversation and focus on the family. "Yes, I suppose we have. So, as much as we don't want to, let's get that box out of the shed down here and show Sissy what we've found."

Sitting on the grass now, the three began inspecting the contents of the box. There were lots of family photos, some taken by Effie, some that had come from their paternal Grandmother Ruth's house. There were copies of property deeds and receipts from about 1959 to 1970.

Margo and Jacob had taken time while Sissy was at the house to inspect the documents, and note any oddities in them. They took turns pointing out things that they had found.   There were the deeds to three hotels, the house in Rochester, Effie's house here, and a house in Savannah GA.   What was odd about these deeds, they pointed out to Sissy, was the change of ownership on them. The originals were deeded to their father, David.   Then in October of 1969, the deeds were transferred to their grandfather, Edward.   Again in the fall of 1970, all of the properties were deeded back to their father - all except one.   The Rochester house was deeded not to David, or his father, but to his mother Ruth that fall of 1970.   In the midst of all of this was a promissory note between David and one Glen Cardinal.   In the note, written in 1969, David had promised to sign over assets to cover "monies owed".   It was very cryptic in that it didn't say how much was owed, or what for.   On the back of the note was "paid in full" written and signed by Mr. Cardinal.   A second promissory note between David, his father Edward, and Effie was written in the same way, only this time with "paid in full" written and signed by Edward.

"What the hell does all this mean?" Sissy was as confused as Jacob and Margo had been. Jacob frowned, "We don't know, it's really weird. I wonder if we can find this Glen Cardinal. Why do you suppose dad had a house in Savannah?" "My guess is that they bought the house that their first apartment was in for sentimental reasons," Sissy reasoned, "I just don't know where to go with all of this." "There's more," Margo added, "we found some weird pictures." She pulled out a pile of pictures for Sissy to examine. Some of the pictures were normal family photos, people smiling and happy. There were, however, several pictures from Ruth's collection where Effie, Jacob, or both of them had been cut out with scissors. There were also pictures from Effie's collection where Edward had been cut out with scissors. "I don't understand this at all," Sissy shook her head, "this is like something out of a freaky suspense movie.   Why would grandma cut Jacob out of some of her pictures, I mean, in most of these, he would have been a baby, and she kept him in some of the pictures once he was older.   Why did she cut out mom during that same time period, and why did mom in turn cut out grandpa?"   "That old bitch has never liked me," Jacob scoffed, "the only one of us she has ever cared about is Margo."   Sissy nodded in agreement, and turned toward Margo.   "I can understand why she was never close to me now.   I was the reason mom and dad got married, and I'm sure she wasn't pleased with that, but what about Jacob? They had been married for eleven years when Jacob was born." Margo shrugged, "I really don't know Sissy. I've always been close to her and she's never said a word about any of this." The siblings sat in silence for a few moments, each of them deep in thought, racking their brains for some kind of logical answers to all of the clues they'd uncovered. They were getting nowhere, and finally Sissy spoke. "Margo, when was the last time you saw or spoke with grandma Ruth?" Margo looked up toward the sky, "I guess it was about a year ago, Marcus and I went and spent a day with her. We were driving to visit you and Jeff, and decided to stop and see her on the way." Sissy had an idea. "Maybe you could call her after

lunch, and ask her about Glen Cardinal?"
Margo nodded in agreement, "I'll do that.
What are we going to do for lunch
anyway?   I don't feel like cooking."
Jacob jumped to his feet, "I'll go to town
and get subs for us!"   He was already
halfway up the incline when Sissy called
out, "Do you think you should drive since
you've been drin…."   She cut herself off
before finishing her thought, he was
ignoring her anyway.   She sighed,
"Idiot."   "He's hurting, Siss, let's cut him
some slack," Margo pleaded.   Sissy bit
her bottom lip, "I know Margo, and
unfortunately, I think it's about to get a
whole lot worse!"

Chapter 14

Two and a half hours had passed, and there was still no sign of Jacob. Sissy and Margo had passed the time by sitting on the dock, listening to the radio. Irritated, Sissy spat, "Where did he go to get subs, New York City?" Margo kept quiet as usual, happily swirling her feet in the water, and bobbing to the music. It was a beautiful, clear afternoon on the lake, and Margo wished silently that Sissy could just enjoy it. "Sissy, if he doesn't come back soon, I'll fix us some lunch, no big deal, okay?" Sissy huffed, "That's not the point Margo. I'm really worried about him!" Margo leaned over and rubbed her sister's back. "He'll be alright, sweetie. Stop worrying about him. He's always been a carefree soul, and done tons of idiotic things, but God has His hand on that stupid boy!" Sissy laughed and thought never a truer statement had been spoken. "Okay Margo, you win. I'll try to be calm. But I still think that he's probably doing something majorly stupid, or he's gotten himself into some kind of trouble!" Margo smiled, "Let's go for a walk around the lake. It's a beautiful day and it will do us both some good. We'll grab some snacks and take them with us."

The walk around the lake was indeed just what Sissy needed. It was nice to enjoy the wildlife and flora, and to see other human beings as they passed by summer homes and campsites. "Isn't it funny," Sissy commented, "I've spent most of my adult life worrying that I've been a huge disappointment to mom, and then we find out that she has this really bizarre, stained past." Margo laughed, "We haven't even uncovered all of the stains, I'm guessing." Both girls were laughing now, thinking of their prudish, church going mother, who constantly lectured them when they were young about being proper young ladies. It seemed funny to imagine all of this puritanical advice being delivered to them by a former teenage prostitute. Sissy sighed, "As much as I want to, it's hard to be angry with her.   I mean, God knows, in spite of everything, she was a good mother."

After walking for about an hour or so, they had circled the lake, and were almost back to their own camp.   They had been talking and laughing, when Margo suddenly paused and exclaimed, "Oh, for the love of God!"   There was Jacob's car, cockeyed in the driveway. He was struggling to get out, obviously hammered.   Clarkie's car pulled in behind him, seconds later.   He threw up his hand in warning, "Clarissa, I've got this.   Go with Margo down to the dock, I'll be along in a minute."   Jacob extended his hand, holding a plastic bag, and almost tumbled over.   "I gottt… the shubssh," he slurred, trying to manage a smile.   It was obvious he couldn't even see straight.   Clarkie grabbed the bag from him, and dragged him to the camper, scolding him the entire way. He opened the camper door and practically threw Jacob in, losing his footing, and almost falling in on top of him.   He could still be heard chastising and yelling at Jacob, even after he had slammed the door. There was a moment of silence, and then an eruption of laughter.   Oddly enough, the laughter was coming from Sissy!

"I'm sorry Margo, I really want to be mad

about this, but that whole scene was just too damned funny!"   Margo smirked, "Do you think we still get to have our 'shubssh'?"   Both girls were hysterically laughing now, holding on to one another, tears streaming down their faces.

The late afternoon sun was heating up anything it touched to the point of discomfort, so the sisters decided to sit in the shade in their folding chairs.   Sipping iced tea, they chattered and laughed like little girls.   The ominous mood that had engulfed the camp earlier had been broken up by the "show" that had been put on by their brother and Clarkie. Both girls were feeling peckish, and were glad to see Clarkie walking down the incline with the subs in hand. Margo tried to stifle a giggle, "So…..what happened Sam?" Clarkie's face was crimson. "I was driving through town on my way here, and saw his rust bucket parked in front of the tavern. I parked beside his car and went inside to find him completely sozzled, going on and on about being the son of a whore to anyone who would listen. I told him that it was time to go and that I'd give him a ride. He agreed, but when we got outside, he jumped into his car, flipped me off, and started driving. I followed him here to make sure he'd be okay. He was driving like a bat out of hell, swerving all over, and narrowly missed a few mailboxes on the way. The little bastard!"   Both girls erupted with laughter, unable to contain it.   After a few moments, Clarkie allowed himself to calm down, and smiled a little.   "I'll tell you what," he gloated, "I think I'll join you ladies in a late lunch.   I'm going to eat the little prick's sub!"

Once they had finished their food, and some small talk was exchanged, Margo decided to get down to business. "Clarkie, do you know who Glen Cardinal is?"   He shrugged, "Of course I do." Margo smiled, "Well what's the deal with him, what's his connection to our family?" She should have known that Clarkie wasn't going to make anything easy for them. "Girls, you know the rules. I'm here to guide and advise, not to tell you the whole story. You're going to have to do your homework on this one." Margo frowned, "Well fine, we will. I have to call grandma Ruth this evening, but I guess that will be hard to do with a drunken idiot passed out in the camper." Clarkie winked, "Actually ladies, I took the liberty of bringing you a cordless phone from your mother's house. I figured that you would want to be able to move about a bit, and sometimes have some privacy." Margo's heart sank a little. She knew that the call was probably not going to be the usual friendly chat she was used to having with her grandmother, and she was looking for any excuse not to have it at all.   "I'll go hook the phone up for you," Clarkie said, and made his way up to the camper.   He returned in five minutes time, and handed the receiver to Margo. She dialed the number and said, "Well, here goes nothing."

  "Hello?"   Ruth always sounded sophisticated, and younger than her 83 years on the phone.   "Hi grandma, it's me."   "Margo!   What a lovely surprise! How are you, darling?"   They had the run of the mill grandmother/granddaughter chat, discussing the Bed and Breakfast, Margo's pregnancy, Ruth's gardens, and of course the weather. Finally, Margo bit the bullet. "Grandma, do you know a man by the name of Glen Cardinal, and if so, do you know how I can reach him?" There was complete silence for a moment, and then, an explosion from the other end of the line. "Don't you EVER speak that filthy name to me again, and if you have questions about him, you'd better take them up with that mother of yours and leave me the hell out of it!" With that, Ruth hung up the phone. Margo's ear was ringing from the volume and tone of her grandmother's voice. "Ok Sissy, what's plan B?"

Chapter 15

Clarkie had made his exit right after polishing off Jacob's food, it pained him to have all of the information the girls were seeking, and not be able to help them. He had made a solemn promise to Effie that other than making contact with Liza to get the ball rolling, he would make the children do the rest on their own. Still, he was secretly trying to come up with ways to bend the rules a little, he just hadn't worked it out yet. Effie was a crafty soul, and she'd know if he butted in more than they'd agreed upon. "I don't know what to tell you Margo. Obviously, you're not going to get much out of

Clarkie or grandma Ruth. Maybe I can call Liza again and see what she will tell me." Sissy really didn't want to intrude on Liza again, but any little tidbit she might get out of her would be worth it. "It's worth a shot I guess," Margo shrugged, "even if we get some idea of who this guy is, where he's from, and if he's even still alive." Sissy nodded, "The way this week's gone so far, maybe it's better if he IS dead. Old ghosts are harder to handle if they aren't actually dead yet."

Sissy took the cordless phone and went to the dock. "Hello," Liza answered right away. "Liza, it's Clarissa. I have some more questions for you." Liza seemed genuinely happy to hear from her young cousin again, and was concerned how everyone was doing considering the blow they'd been dealt. After exchanging some pleasantries, Sissy got down to business. "Liza, I need to know who Glen Cardinal is. Do you know anything about him?" Liza was silent for a moment. "Darlin', of course I know who he is. But you know that I can't really tell you everything I know about him. Your mother…" "Yes I know," Sissy flushed, "I know mother has set all of these rules for everyone. I just need the basics Liza. We need to find him, or someone who knows him. We need to close this hellish chapter in our lives so that we can all go home and have some peace!" Liza sighed, "Child, 'closing this chapter' as you call it, will bring you anything but peace! You will have to find your own peace after all of this, seek after it wherever you believe you'll find it. What I can tell you, is that you won't find it in knowledge...at least not the knowledge you're after." Liza went on to give Sissy what little bits of information she could, and Sissy thanked her profusely. As they were ending their conversation, Liza said, "How's that boy?" Sissy frowned, "You mean Jacob?" "Yes lamb, that's who I meant. You and your sister hold tight to that boy, y'hear?" and with that, Liza hung up the phone.

Margo had been tidying up the campsite while Sissy was on the phone. It was nearly five o'clock, and she figured eventually they'd want to make a plan for dinner. She was sitting by the fire with a glass of iced tea when Sissy joined her. "She would only give bare minimum information," Sissy lit a cigarette, "Mother has tied her hands also." Margo's face reddened, "Damn mother! Why did she take the coward's way out? She could have told us the truth to our faces, let us have a chance to ask some questions!" Sissy stifled a giggle, amused by Margo's sudden outburst. "Yes, but Margo, as sickening as it was to find out what mother was in her past, we have no idea what else we will find. I'm angry with her too, but God knows we can't really blame her for hiding.   I mean, think about it, her whole life has been a lie from the beginning!   She's a Jew who was raised in a Presbyterian church.   Talk about learning to playact from the get go!" Margo began to calm down a little. Sissy was right, their mother's foundation had always been built on sand.   "So what do we know about Glen Cardinal, Siss?"   Sissy frowned, "Not much, unfortunately.   He was an acquaintance and drinking buddy of dad's.   He owns a hotel in the Adirondack's.   According to Liza, he comes from old money, and drinks and gambles more than he actually works.   He has only ever been able hold on to that one hotel, which he inherited, and I guess he was always jealous of daddy's success.   I'm speculating they were probably not true friends, more like two men in the same line of work, who both liked to drink and gamble.   But this is all third hand information, from mother to Liza, then Liza to me.   That's all she would give me, and I'm not sure what to do with it."   Margo scratched her chin, "Do you mind if I give Marcus a call? Maybe he can give us some advice on how to proceed with all of this."   Sissy nodded, "I'm going to take another walk, you call Marcus.   When I get back, we should probably try to wake up the little turd that's snoring in the camper."   Both girls laughed, and Margo went off to the dock to retrieve the cordless and call her husband.

Sissy walked along the lake path, allowing herself to daydream. She remembered happier days, she and Margo swimming in the lake as little girls before Jacob was born. "A lot of things seemed happier before Jacob was born," she thought to herself, guilt falling on her once the thought had processed. But the more she thought about it, the more she wondered just what it was about Jacob coming along that had caused such a change in the family. It was almost as if lightning had struck the very soul of the Banks clan. She had often thought that maybe it was because Jacob was born so many years after she and Margo, but now as she thought about it more extensively, the age gap really wasn't that big of a deal. Effie was only

28 when Jacob was born, so it wasn't as if he was one of those "change of life" babies that everyone talked about. "There's something more, something about Jacob that is different," she said out loud to herself.   She walked on, letting her thoughts go to Jeff.   She knew in her heart, that she had poisoned their marriage slowly, over the past few years. This baggage that they were all uncovering had always been a part of her whether she'd acknowledged it or not, and she had allowed it to taint everything and everyone she loved.   She stopped at an empty camp, went to the shore, and skipped some rocks across the surface, something she hadn't done in years. She could see the dock of the Banks camp from where she was, and she

sighed. A frog perched on a lily pad close by let out a loud croak, and she said, "I know, I know. It's time to go back."

It was after six o'clock when Sissy stepped onto the lot. She was startled when suddenly, the camper door flew open, crashing into the outside wall of the camper. There was Jacob, on his hands and knees puking his guts out. "Hey bro," she said nonchalantly and continued down to the lower half of the camp. He wasn't going to get any sympathy out of her.

Margo was by the fire, reading a magazine. "Hey! How was your walk?" Sissy smiled. "It was nice. The jackass is up there heaving all over the place." Both girls laughed. "Serves him right," Margo said, "but somehow I think he'll be down shortly for another beer." They sat in silence for a moment, both enjoying the breeze. "So here's what Marcus suggested. We need to go online and see if we can find Mr. Cardinal using the small amount of information we have. We can go to the library tomorrow when it opens, or Marcus said there's a new cyber cafe in town that he and Jeff passed when they went out to get out groceries. We could go tonight if you want, it might be open." Sissy smiled, "Let's go to town just to check it out. We can pick up some Chinese food to bring back for ourselves and "boy wonder". His keys are in my purse, so he won't be able to be a public menace while we're gone."

The drive into town was just what the doctor ordered.   The girls laughed, sang along to the radio, and reminisced about drives they had taken together when Sissy had first obtained her driver's license.   "I don't know where this stupid cafe is Margo.   I didn't notice it the last time I was here."   Margo laughed, "It's a tiny village with two traffic lights, how hard can it be to find?"   They looked in both directions, driving down the main street. "Look Siss, there it is!"   Right where "Hardy's Liquor" had been when they were kids, was a shiny neon sign which simply read "Cyber Cafe".   Sissy smirked. Moments later, they were ordering fancy overpriced coffees and paying for their internet usage.   The cafe was warm and inviting, with cushy chairs, and new age music playing quietly in the background. None of this appealed to Sissy, who was in no mood to get comfortable here. "We have a half hour of internet time, let's find what we can find, and get outta Dodge!"   Within twenty minutes, Margo had some solid leads to work with, they had finished their coffee's, and were out the door.

The Chinese restaurant was just as both girls had remembered. It had changed hands a few times over the years, but the restaurant itself was still the same: four small booths on either side with paper menu place mats, gaudy dragons on the walls, a large lit up menu with pictures of food above the register, and a small Buddhist shrine at the register with oranges, incense, and a tiny fountain. They ordered dinners for themselves and Jacob to go, the cashier responding, "Ten-fifteen minute." Sissy laughed, "Why is it that you can go to any Chinese restaurant in the country, and the wait is always 'ten-fifteen minute'?" Margo blushed, stifling a giggle. Sissy cracked open a fortune cookie and read the paper inside. It read, "many changes coming your way". Sissy's tone of voice dripped with sarcasm, "Oh, REALLY??" Once they had food in hand, they were on their way back to the lake. Margo looked concerned. "I don't think I'm ready for what we may find out from this Glen Cardinal." Sissy nodded, "I don't think we have a choice anymore."

Chapter 16

The girls pulled into the lake lot and noticed that Jacob had made his way down to the fire pit. Even from a distance, they could see that he looked indignant. Margo frowned, "What's he got to be mad about?" "Who knows," Sissy replied, "probably because I took his keys." They gathered the papers that Margo had printed off at the cyber cafe, and the food, and made their way down to face whatever tongue lashing Jacob would hand out.

It seemed that the alcohol had mostly dissipated from Jacob's system, but was replaced by ire. "What the hell's the meaning of you two sneaking off and leaving me here? You could have at least told me where you were going, or asked if I wanted to come along!" Margo took the reigns, "It's not our fault that you drank yourself completely stupid, and missed the whole afternoon snoring in the camper! Why would we want you to come with us, so we could smell your boozy breath and listen to your childish whining the whole way? And listen, I'm gonna be a mom, but I'm not YOUR mom, and I'm not about to take care of you when you're vomiting in the car!" Jacob set his jaw and narrowed his eyes, "And which one of you took my car keys?

You had no right to do that!"   Sissy had heard enough.   "I took them, you don't need to be driving around drunk!   Now, go jump in the lake, get another beer, or whatever it is you have to do to calm down, but quit being a little dick because we aren't going to tolerate it!"   He softened, realizing like he always did when he drank too much that he had crossed the line.   "I'm sorry guys.   I'm going to go out on the dock and have a smoke."   The girls shared a muffled giggle, and sat near the fire to get ready to eat.   When Jacob came back from his cigarette break, the girls had the food all laid out with paper plates and silverware for all.   "Get any chopsticks?"   Jacob was smiling now, feeling better.   Sissy smiled, "Of course brat.   We know you like them."   The three sat and ate in silence.   There was a lot to say, but these days there was no such thing as casual conversation in the Banks camp.

Jacob, having finished his food, playfully tossed the paper plate and plastic cutlery into the fire.   It was something they would have been punished for as children. The girls laughed, and followed suit, thick black smoke emanating from the burning plastic.   "I'm going to get a beer," Jacob chortled, "you want one, Sis?"   She didn't have to think long after the day she'd had.   "Yes, I want one, and then lets get down to business."

Bellies full, and Sissy and Jacob half way through a beer, Margo began to reiterate what she'd found.

"So here's what we have.   Glen Cardinal owns the Cardinal Hotel in Lake George, NY.   Most of the hotels up there are seasonal, and shut down for the winter, but the Cardinal has an extensive business center, and a lot of other attractive amenities, so they operate year round.   The hotel has a large banquet hall,and two restaurants, one of which provides catering.   Mr. Cardinal owned several other hotels previously, but they have all since gone defunct.   He is listed in the phone book, but the number given is the same number as the hotel.   I think that we should try a call tonight and see if we can reach him."   Sissy chimed in, "I agree.   And because we've done most of the leg work on this, I think you should be the one to call, Jacob."   Jacob frowned, "I suppose you're right, but let's call in the morning."   "No dice," Margo replied, "We need answers sooner rather than later."

Jacob cracked another beer. He had always struggled with anxiety, and had erroneously learned to self medicate himself with alcohol. If ever there was a time to drink, he reasoned, it was now. Wetting his lips and clearing his throat, he dialed the number. The voice that answered on the other end was pleasant and professional. "Good evening, and thank you for calling the Cardinal Hotel, Erica speaking. How may I help you?" Jacob was sweating profusely. "I'm looking for your manager I guess, Glen Cardinal. May I speak to him?" There was a slight pause on the other end, "I'm sorry sir, she's with a guest right now, would you like to hold, or would you like me to put you through to her voicemail?" "I'm sorry, you must have misunderstood,

I'm looking for Glen Cardinal, the hotel manager." Another slight pause, "Yes sir, as I said, she's with a guest right now. Would you like her voicemail?" "No, thanks." Jacob quickly hung up the phone. "What just happened," Sissy asked, "is he not there or something?" Jacob downed the rest of his beer. "I don't know quite how to tell you this, but HE is a SHE." Margo shook her head, "No, that's not possible. Nothing we found indicates that Glen Cardinal is a female. That makes absolutely no sense at all." Jacob opened another beer. "Margo, you or Sissy can call back if you want, but I'm not doing it! I already feel like a giant ass!" "You ARE a giant ass," Sissy retorted, "give me the phone and I'll call myself." She lit a cigarette, and dialed the phone. "Good evening, and thank you for calling the Cardinal Hotel, Erica speaking. How may I help you?" "Hello, I'm trying to get in touch with your manager, Glen Cardinal. Is he available?" "I'm sorry ma'am, but she's with a guest at the moment. Would you like to hold, or shall I put you through to her voicemail?" Sissy hung up abruptly, and looked at Margo. "Shit."

Chapter 17

"Guys, we can't just continue to hang up on this poor woman, whoever she is. Give me the phone."   Margo was tired of going in circles.   "I'm going to call and see if we can get to the bottom of this." The phone rang, and Margo received the same scripted oratory that Jacob and Sissy had heard, but instead of hanging up she said, "Yes, I'd be glad to hold." Sissy and Jacob were on the edge of their chairs, wide eyed, anxious, almost as if they were waiting to open their gifts on Christmas morning.   Between her siblings observing her like an animal in a cage, and the fact that someone had taken one of her favorite pop songs and turned it into saxophone hold music, Margo was starting to feel vexed. "Will you two go to the dock or something, you're driving me nuts! When I actually get her on the phone, I'll let you know." Sissy and Jacob reluctantly made their way out to the dock. Jacob lit the lanterns and citronella candles. It wasn't dark yet, but he knew it would be soon, and he didn't want to fumble around in the dark later to light them. Minutes later, they could see from the dock that Margo was talking to someone on the phone. Jacob jumped up and Sissy grabbed his arm. "Leave her. If we go over there and try to listen in, she'll lose her train of thought. It'll make her nervous, and she already has pregnancy brain. When she's done talking, we'll go back."   Jacob was mildly irritated, he wasn't much for boundaries, but had to admit to himself that what Sissy had said made sense. Meanwhile, sitting by the fire, Margo was sorting things out.

"So you are Glen Cardinal?"   The polite,feminine voice on the other end answered affirmatively.   Margo's face burned with embarrassment.   "I was looking for a Glen Cardinal that was an old acquaintance of my father's.   My father, David Banks, was a hotel owner, and he and the Glen I'm looking for used to drink and gamble together.   I'm sorry to have bothered you, ma'am."   There was laughter on the other end of the line. "You haven't bothered me at all!   I am Glenna Cardinal, Glen is my father. Daddy was so sure that I was going to be a boy, the only name my parents had picked out was Glen Jr.   As I am obviously not a boy, I was dubbed Glenna, but everyone has always called me Glen. I have always worked for daddy, and took over as manager of the hotel four years ago when his health took a bad turn." Margo was relieved, and allowed herself to laugh.   "So, I hate to be a nuisance, but where is your father now?   I have some questions for him regarding my mother and father.   Apparently, some of my father's properties changed hands back and forth some years ago while they were gambling together."   Glen chuckled a bit, "It really doesn't surprise me.   My father is a great man, but he's terrible with business, and has always had a fondness for drinking and gambling.   I've heard him speak of your father many times Ms. Banks, and it's always been hard to decipher if they were good friends, or hated one another."   Margo wanted to say that she had ceased to be "Ms. Banks" two years ago when she became "Mrs. Bellows", but decided that in this instance, it was a minor detail that could be ironed out later.   "Is there a number I can reach him at, Ms. Cardinal?   I'd really like to speak with him."   There was a slight pause on the other end of the line. "Please, call me Glen.   Daddy lives here at the hotel, in one of the suites.   He doesn't go out, and I doubt that he would talk on the phone.   He developed cirrhosis, which in turn has developed into hepatic cancer.   He's been kind of a bitter old man for the last five years." Margo sighed, "And you, please, call me Margo.   This is unfortunate, I really need to speak to your dad.   My siblings and I are trying to sort some family mysteries out, and I think your father has some pieces of the puzzle."   "I'll tell you what I can do, Margo.   You and your siblings are more than welcome to come up here and stay in one of our rooms as my guests.   Once you get here, I will go with you to talk to daddy and try to soften him up a bit.   About how far of a drive is it for you?"   Margo thought for a moment, "It's about three hours I think.   I wonder if it would be better if just one of us comes, that way your father won't feel bombarded."   "Sounds good Margo. One of you can come tonight, if you feel like it's not too late, or you can plan on coming tomorrow."   "Glen, I think one of us leaving in the morning is probably better.   I don't know who will come at this point, we'll have to hash out the details, may I call you in the morning and let you know?"   Glen smiled, "Of course you may.   I live here at the hotel also, so I will give you my personal number to call and I will also let my staff know to find me immediately if you call the front desk." Margo felt suddenly comfortable with this stranger whom she'd never laid eyes on.

"Thank you so much Glen!   We'll be in touch tomorrow morning."

After hanging up, Margo decided to place a call to Clarkie, before her siblings realized that she was off the phone and pounced on her.   "Clarkie, one of us has to go to Lake George tomorrow, and speak with Glen Cardinal in person.   I'm not sure who's going to go, but will you be the driver?"   "Of course I will.   I don't suggest that you send Jacob, he'll just get into trouble with his mouth and his boozing.   You're probably the most level headed, and the best candidate to go, but just check with your sister, and I'll be there at eight o'clock to take whoever is going.   Will we be staying the night?" Margo was getting a bit of a headache at this point.   "I don't know, lets just plan on it being an overnight trip, and if it turns out to be just a day trip, then no harm done.   I think that Sissy will agree with you and want to send me.   Will you call Ms. Cardinal back and let her know that you'll be there tomorrow around eleven with Mrs. Margo Bellows?   Maybe if her old man hears a last name other than Banks, he won't shoot us on the spot!" Clarkie laughed, "I'll take care of it.   See you in the morning."

Margo hung up the phone, and waddled out to the dock.   The sun was setting, leaving a beautiful view of the rolling hills in the distance.   "Okay guys, here's what I found out."   She told them everything she had learned on the phone, and explained that one of them would be leaving with Clarkie in the morning. Naturally, Jacob wanted to go, he loved any chance to stay at a hotel, and check out all of the local pubs in a new town. He scowled when he was told that nobody really thought him the best candidate to go.   "You should go, Margo," Sissy decided, "I'll help you pack in case you stay the night.   You will be a fine ambassador for us, God knows at this point you have more tact than Jacob or I put together!"   Margo laughed,

"Probably true.   I only have one request. I need you both to be sober when I get back.   I don't think that this man is going to be particularly pleased with talking to me, and I think that he is going to give us a lot of information that we don't necessarily want to know."   In spite of the warm temperature of the evening, Margo suddenly felt chilled to the bone.

Chapter 18

After a fitful sleep, Margo awakened at
six o'clock.   She felt slightly nauseated,
a feeling she had gotten used to since
finding out she was pregnant, but there
was an added feeling of anxiety that she
wasn't used to.   Normally, Margo was
unusually calm under fire, but not today.
She left her sleeping siblings in the tent,
and made her way to the fire to start the
coffee and get all of her pans and utensils
ready to make breakfast.   She cursed
under her breath as she picked up all of
the beer bottles carelessly left behind by
her brother.   Once she felt that the
campsite was tidy enough, she made her

way to the dock with her coffee. It was a cool morning, fog rolling in off of the lake. Even at home, Margo always enjoyed being the first one awake, being able to just be still and mentally prepare for whatever she had planned for the day. Her thoughts wandered this morning to their mother. Where was Effie? Was she okay? Margo dismissed this line of thought and shook her head, of course Effie was fine. She probably knew everything that her children had been doing, with her network of "spies". Margo chuckled to herself as she doubted that Clarkie would tell their mother about almost landing on his fat ass trying to wrangle a drunken Jacob into the camper. She sat there, quietly, for about a half hour enjoying her coffee and watching the lake wake up along with her.   The finches were singing their morning songs, fish jumped trying to catch fat dragonflies, and frogs bellowed at each other from the comfort of their lily pads.   Margo sighed. She could stay here in this moment forever, but she knew it was time to make breakfast and wake the others.

Margo was a master at cooking, a skill that came in handy when she married the man of her dreams, who just so happened to own a Bed and Breakfast. This morning she prepared beautiful, thick wedges of french toast, spicy turkey sausage patties, fluffy scrambled eggs with smoked cheddar cheese, and real maple syrup infused with orange rind and cinnamon sticks.   She crept to the entrance of the tent and whispered, "Sissy, are you awake?"   She was perfectly fine with letting Jacob sleep in, and having a little "adult" conversation.

Sissy emerged moments later, her hair in a messy bun on top of her head, her eye makeup smeared.   Margo laughed. "Aren't you a vision this morning?"   "Shut it," Sissy giggled, "where's my coffee? You don't wake a girl up and not offer her coffee." Margo handed her a large mug, "Way ahead of you. Breakfast is all done, I have it in pans on the side of the fire to stay warm. Do you want to go out on the dock and talk before "ding-a-ling" wakes up?" Sissy laughed, "That poor boy get's called everything but Jacob these days. Yeah, we'll go out there, and I can have a cigarette." Once they were seated on the dock, and Sissy was a bit more awake, she could see that Margo was visibly nervous. She patted her arm, "What's got you so worked up this morning, love?" Margo sighed, "I'm just afraid that we're going to find out something dreadful. Wouldn't you think that finding out your mother was a prostitute would be the end of the story? Apparently, it's not in our case, and I can't imagine what fresh hell lies behind door number two!"   Sissy fought the urge to laugh at her sister's game show reference, and hugged her tightly.   "Whatever it is, we'll get through it together!   In a weird way, this has been good for us all, brought us closer together.   I can even spend time with the brat now without continually wanting to punch him in the throat!"   Margo burst out laughing.   "Do you remember when he was two, and we put him down the third floor laundry chute? Thank God there was plenty of laundry at the bottom!   I don't think mom had ever, or has ever been as furious as she was that day!"   Both girls howled with laughter at the memory.   Suddenly, muffled in the tent, they heard, "What the hell are you two caterwauling about out there?"   With that, their laughter escalated, Margo pinching her thighs together so as not to wet her pants. Sissy composed herself, "Jacob, I'm going to get you a coffee.   Get out here and have a cigarette with me, and then we'll have breakfast."   Margo looked at her watch.   "It's quarter to seven, so you guys hang out for a bit here on the dock, but we need to eat breakfast soon."

Margo busied herself with packing her personals, while Jacob and Sissy had their coffee and smoke on the dock. Jacob seemed extra irritable this morning.

Sissy sighed, "Okay, I already dealt with "Nervous Nellie" over there, now I guess I get to move on to you. So what's up your ass this morning?" Jacob glared at her. "I just want out of here. I don't know what the point of any of this is now. So we found out mom has a shady past, and I'm trying to deal with that. But I'm assuming that whatever Margo finds out today is going to be about dad, since it's one of his cronies she's going to meet with, and why would I care about that? He never cared about me!" Sissy put her hand on his back. "Do you really believe that? I mean, truly in your heart believe that dad didn't love you?" "Yes, I do! He never showed me the same affection he showed you and Margo. Do you remember the time I got a "C" on a math test in the fifth grade?   He kicked me so hard in the ass that I couldn't walk normally, and mom had to keep me out of school "sick" for two days!"   Sissy's heart sank.   "No Jacob, I'm sorry, I didn't know that.   I was in college then, remember?"   A single tear fell down Jacob's cheek.   "He told me more than once that I was a disgrace to the Banks name, and how if it wasn't for mother, he'd have sent me away."   He was sobbing uncontrollably now, and all Sissy could do was hold him and rock him like a baby.   How had she never known this?   The scenario that Jacob was presenting sounded like outright abuse.   She felt bile rising in the back of her throat, anger smoldering in her belly like a furnace.   After a few moments, Jacob had calmed himself

down, and reached for another cigarette.
Sissy brushed his hair out of his face.
"Listen, I'm going to go have breakfast
with Margo before she has to leave.
You take as much time as you need to
out here, and then join us if you want.
When she's gone, we'll think of
something fun to do today.   Maybe we'll
go take a piss on daddy's grave."   The
last part was completely out of character
for her, and she threw it in at the last
minute just to make him laugh.   It
worked.

Over breakfast, with Jacob still out on the dock, Sissy gave Margo the details of their conversation.   Margo frowned. "Daddy was always kind of a bully to Jacob.   I don't remember seeing anything like he described, but I do remember him being out of school for two days, and walking really funny for a while after that.   I've always thought that the reason Jacob drinks so much is because daddy was so hard on him, and mom tried to compensate by coddling him. Jacob has a very caring nature, he is a natural with elderly people.   He wanted to go to college for nursing when he graduated high school, but daddy had a fit about it, and insisted that he had to go for some kind of business degree. That's why Jacob dropped out, he hated it.

Jacob is really very artistic also, and I remember daddy used to make fun of him for that too, calling him a "pansy". He sends Marcus and I some of his paintings once in a while, and they're beautiful. We hang them in the guest rooms at the Bed and Breakfast. In fact, the painting that you see in the guest room featured in our brochure was done by Jacob!" Sissy gasped, "Really? I love that painting! How did I not know any of this? Now I feel awful." Margo smiled, "Don't feel awful. Just try to get to know him better now, build a relationship with him." Sissy beamed, "Well I did offer to piss on daddy's grave with him today, that's a start, isn't it?" Margo looked momentarily appalled, then both girls were rolling with laughter again. In the distance, they heard a vehicle, and seconds later saw Clarkie pull in.

"Party's over," Margo said, and made her way up the incline to meet him.

Chapter 19

Clarkie had arrived at the lake a little earlier than planned, but Margo was packed, and eager to get on the road. After saying goodbye to her siblings, she belted herself in and said a silent prayer that God would give her the strength to deal with whatever today would bring. Sissy had asked her earlier how she planned to get through a three hour drive alone with Clarkie.   "My doctor gave me medicine for nausea when I was having morning sickness.   It knocks me out, so I'm just going to take one when I get in the car!"   She had done just that, and was asleep before they had even gotten out of town and on the highway.   Clarkie didn't mind, he was used to being alone in a car.   He listened to the national news, and took in the scenery around him.

Margo awakened when they were about thirty miles from Lake George.   She marveled at the beauty of the Adirondack region, and silently wished that this were a vacation instead of a dreadful mission to find out God knows what. She fixed her hair and makeup in the mirror, wanting to look her best as she was meeting these people for the first time. She had chosen to wear a classy summer maternity dress, one she had brought with her in case she and Marcus went out to dinner while they were visiting. It was strapless, knee length, cream colored with little cherries and red trim, and she wore it with red strappy sandals. Clarkie watched her fiddling in the mirror and asked, "Are you nervous?" Margo blinked, "Uh, yeah, aren't you?" He laughed, "Why would I be? I know these people, remember?" She frowned, "Oh, that's right. You could have just told us everything from the get go and saved us all of this grief!" "Margo, there is nothing that you've learned or will learn that I would have had the guts or the heart to tell you." They finished the drive in silence.

Margo was amazed with the amount of tourists packed into the quaint little town of Lake George. "Marcus and I could have a little B&B here if we ever decided to move back north!" Clarkie grinned, "You're forgetting that they practically roll the sidewalks up in the wintertime." Just minutes away from town, they took a sharp left onto a road that seemed to

Margo to be headed straight up the mountain.   Her ears popped from the change in altitude, and the twists and turns in the road were beginning to make her sick.   After what seemed like an eternity, they pulled up to the hotel. Margo gasped, "My God!"   The looming building ahead looked more like a European palace than an upstate New York hotel.   The valet greeted them warmly, "Hello Mr. Clark, always so nice to see you!   It's a pleasure to meet you Mrs. Bellows.   Ms. Cardinal is expecting you both in her private lounge for cocktail hour."   Margo gave a sideways glance at Clarkie.   "Cocktail hour?   It's not even noon yet, and I'm pregnant."   Clarkie grinned, "I'm not pregnant!   Really Margo, obviously there will be nonalcoholic refreshments for you." She softened, realizing that she was taking her nervousness out on Clarkie. "How often do you come up here, Sam?" He laughed. "Let's just say that in the last few years, I've been here more than I wanted to be."

They made their way into the lobby, and once Margo's eyes adjusted from being out in the sun, she was awed by what she saw: marble floors and fireplaces, mahogany woodwork and columns, silk covered walls, velvet drapes, and fresh cut flowers arranged in crystal vases.   This indeed was more like a palace, something out of the "Gilded Age" of America, a time when the very rich and elite had family homes as opulent as this hotel.   "Follow me," Clarkie said, and headed to a small elevator off in a corner that was marked "staff only".   The old elevator opened to a much smaller lobby, where they were greeted by a secretary in a smart, pin striped suit.   "Hello again, Mr. Clark.   Mrs. Bellows, I'm Marsha, one of Ms. Cardinal's personal secretaries.   Please make your way to the double doors on the left where Ms. Cardinal is waiting in the lounge.   I hope you'll enjoy your visit here, and I will be personally overseeing your stay here.   I trust you'll let me know if there is anything you need while you are here."

Once inside the double doors, they were in the "inner sanctum", the private lounge. There was a full bar with a bartender, several comfortable tables, couches and overstuffed chairs accompanied by coffee tables, and a game room off to the side with pool tables and dart boards.   Near the back of the lounge, standing by the door to the private kitchen, was a waiter an a busboy.   "I could get used to this," Margo thought, and then felt a hand on her shoulder.   Nearly jumping out of her skin, she turned to see a beautiful woman that reminded her a little bit of Sissy. Glenna "Glen" Cardinal stood at 5'11", with long strawberry blonde hair that she kept in a french twist, high cheekbones, creamy complexion, steel grey eyes, a long bridged nose that turned up at the tip, and bow shaped lips that were painted the color of a fine merlot. "I'm so sorry I frightened you, Margo!" Her voice was rich and clear like a cello. Margo blushed, and the ladies exchanged a handshake. Glen motioned toward a table, "Let's have a seat. Smitty will take our order and we can have some refreshments." Clarkie and Glen each ordered a cocktail, Margo asked for a diet cola with lime. "So Margo, let's get to what brought you here. You need to speak to my father, correct?" Margo reached for her purse. "I do. I have many questions for him about these papers that my siblings and I found, and what they all mean." She fumbled in her purse to produce the papers, but paused as she felt Glen's hand on her arm.

"You won't need any of your papers.   My father has a keen memory when it comes to the past, especially if it involves any kind of rivalry, or if he feels he's been wronged in any way."   Glen took a sip of her scotch.   "Daddy is brilliant, a visionary, and could have had all the success in the world.   His downfall is his drinking and gambling.   He's also selfish, competitive, possessive, irrational, and manipulative.   My mother left when I was three, she couldn't deal with him any longer.   She didn't dare take me with her for fear that he would find a way to punish her for it, and I haven't seen her since. He and your father had some sort of dispute nearly thirty years ago, he's never given me the details.   Oddly enough, shortly after your father's death, he started locking himself in the office, drinking all day and all night.   It was then that I persuaded him to hand over the management of the hotel completely to me.   He's lived in the penthouse suite ever since, I can rarely get him to venture out.   He sits up there drinking and mumbling to himself all day long.   The doctors have suggested that he may suffer from PTSD, but I have no idea what could have caused something like that.   Sounds like a peach, doesn't he?" Margo swallowed hard, "And...he's agreed to meet with me today?"   Glen chuckled, "I told him he was meeting with a Mrs. Bellows today, a representative for the Banks family estate.   Have no fear, he can smell bullshit a mile away, and as soon as you go in there, he'll know who you are.   I'll go with you, and if he refuses to talk, I'll threaten to take all of his booze away.   He is petrified of leaving that suite, so threatening to remove all of the alcohol always works when I need him to cooperate."   Margo frowned, "I'm sorry Glen, but this is absolutely dreadful!   I feel as though I'd rather face a firing squad than go up there!"   Glen threw her head back and laughed, "I feel the same way every time I go up there.   Unfortunately, it may be the only way you can find the answers you're looking for."   Margo brushed beads of sweat from her forehead.   "I'm afraid you're right.   So what now?"   "Well... now, Sam and I down another drink, you say a quiet prayer, and we all head up to the lion's den!"

Chapter 20

After stepping off of the private elevator from the lounge, Glen led the way through the main lobby, and far down a corridor containing mostly staff offices and closets.   "There's only one elevator that goes all the way up to daddy's suite. I had it installed about two years ago, and had the other elevators remodeled and configured to only go as far as the floor below it."   They arrived at the small elevator, and Glen further explained, "There's a code for the elevator that only select staff members have access to.   I have to restrict who goes up there.   I don't trust my dad, and I don't want him conducting illegal activities inside of this hotel.   I've worked hard to change it from an underground gambling den to an upscale and reputable hotel."   The three got on, and as the elevator lurched slowly upward, Margo suddenly wished there was an escape hatch.   After what seemed an eternity, the elevator stopped, and the doors opened.   There was a lobby area outside of the door of the suite, just as grand as the main lobby, only on a smaller scale.   Here, there were two couches, a love seat, three plush chairs, a small wishing well fountain, and several lush potted palms.   An enormous skylight, high in the ceiling above, brought in natural sunlight, and the warmth from it. "I could live right here," Margo blurted out, then blushed from embarrassment.

Glen laughed, "When daddy is in one of his particularly harsh moods, I post two male employees out here for the night just to listen in, and make sure he doesn't hurt himself, so I want them to be comfortable. He always knows when they're here, and often invites them in when he gets tired of drinking alone. I don't really mind as long as I know that he's safe. You ready to face the music, Margo?" "No, I'm not. But I must." Glen knocked on the door, and then immediately opened it, not waiting for an invitation.

The suite appeared as if it were once elaborate, elegant, and beautiful, but had since been overtaken by an alcoholic hoarder.   There were boxes strewn everywhere, broken glass on the floor, empty liquor bottles in the potted plants, and piles of papers in every corner.   In the middle of the room, facing the door, was a single couch surrounded by black garbage bags, candy bar wrappers, and peanut shells.   On the center cushion of the couch sat the man that Margo had come to see.   The Sr. Glen Cardinal was in a brown suit that looked as if it had been tailored in the 1970's, and possibly worn continuously since that time.   His greasy white hair, gaunt cheeks, swollen body, and long yellowed fingernails almost made him look like a monster out of a black and white horror movie. Margo could hardly believe that this man was only sixty years old, his body ravaged by years of chemical abuse. "Daddy, so glad to see that you're eating," Glenna smirked, and eyed the candy wrappers and peanut shells. His laugh was thick, guttural, as monstrous as the man himself. "Such a witty girl I've raised. Pity you can't seem to find a man content with leaving his balls in your purse! Maybe you're a lesbian, I always did figure that your mother was one." Glenna completely ignored his insults, she was used to this game. "Daddy, this is Mrs. Bellows, the lady that I told you would be coming." Margo forced herself to smile and said, "Hello." He sneered at Margo, "Bellows, huh? Bellows my ass!

You're a Banks!   I can see Esther in those eyes of yours, and you've got your father's idiotic grin.   Bellows….what kind of a name is Bellows?   Irish, or English maybe?   Certainly not a surname you would expect the daughter of a slimy charlatan and a kike Mississippi whore to have!"   Clarkie's eyes were the size of dinner plates, and Glenna seemed to be scanning the room looking for an escape route.   To everyone's astonishment, Margo let out a small chuckle.   "Is that all you've got old man?   Really?   I come all the way here for the truth, and you think you're going to scare me away… by speaking the truth?   I am what you described, what of it?   You, on the other hand, are a bitter, tragic, broken down, bloated booze bag, with a filthy mouth, and shitty disposition.   So I guess now we've both spoken our truth, and I'll just leave you to rot in this tomb that you've created for yourself.   I'll get answers one way or another before I set foot off of this property, whether it's you that gives them to me or not!   Lovely to have met you." She turned on her heels, and started toward the door.   "No wait!   Come back! I've misjudged you, little girl.   I didn't think you'd be able to handle the knowledge that you've come here to collect today, but you've just proven that you certainly can!   Glenna, go get this girl a comfortable chair to sit in, and then you and Mr. Clark get your asses out of here!   And send one of your slave boys up here with something decent for her to eat and drink.   All I have is hooch, and

she's obviously in the family way."
Glenna retrieved one of the cushioned
chairs from the tiny outside lobby, and
brought it in for Margo.   Clarkie, who had
been too stunned to move, was now
fidgeting, shifting his weight from one foot
to the other.   "Sam and I will be right
outside the door Margo, you yell if you
need us."   Clarkie spoke up, "I'm staying
right here.   I need to make sure Margo is
alright."   The old man leaned forward
and hissed, "You heard me!   We don't
need a crooked lawyer for this meeting,
now piss off!"   Margo nodded toward the
door and smiled, "I'll be fine, Clarkie, go."

Now that it was just the two of them, Margo saw a sudden change in Glen's disposition. He was softer somehow, almost gentle. "I'm assuming dear, since you weren't shocked by my description of your parents, that you've already heard the tale of how they met and married?" She nodded and smiled, "Yes, old news." He shook his head and chuckled, "You know Margo, I haven't had a decent visitor in years, just those lackeys that my daughter sends up here when I'm throwing a fit. I do that just to be a pain in her ass, I'm not really crazy." Margo laughed, "I think that it's possible that you are slightly crazy, if we're still telling the truth." They both laughed. "By golly, Margo, you've got one hell of a personality, you're a real classy dame. I think I'll break out the champagne.   Will you join me in one?"   Margo paused, but remembered that her obstetrician had told her that a glass of wine once in a while when she couldn't sleep would be okay. She answered, "Why not?"   He left the room for a moment, and came back brandishing two crystal flukes of champagne.

"I'll start, Margo, by apologizing for my crude description of your mother.   I am, as you said, a bitter old man.   I met your mother in 1964, and fell instantly, madly in love with her.   She was only 22 then, but already had your sister and yourself. There was something in those eyes of hers.   It was as if she carried the centuries long struggle of the Jewish nation right there in her eyes.   I had been an acquaintance of your father for a couple of years beforehand.   I'm sure you already know, our mutual interests were boozing and gambling.

Underground gambling was big in those days, and everyone wanted a piece of the pie.   My father was still alive then, but had handed the management of this hotel over to me.   He and my mother spent most of their time in Florida, semi-retired. So I planned a long weekend of gambling, and invited some heavy hitters that I knew had the money to really play.   Your father was one of those people, and he and your mother came and spent the weekend.   She went sightseeing with you girls, played with you in the pool, and stayed with you in the suite while your father and I got drunk and gambled with my other guests.   It was a fun weekend, and we all promised to get together and do it again some other time."   He paused, coughed a few times, and then fumbled in his filthy jacket pocket for a cigarette. Margo sipped her champagne, dreading whatever was coming next.

"I saw your parent's from time to time over the next couple of years, at functions that we would mutually attend, but it wasn't until the fall of 1969 that they returned here for a weekend. While your father was rubbing elbows with my other guests, and gearing up for a weekend of boozing and gambling, I had a cocktail with your mother at the bar. She confided in me that your father was the love of her life, but that they had become estranged. The mixture of his gambling, drinking, and his controlling parents had taken a toll on the marriage, and that summer they had started sleeping in separate bedrooms. She said that she would do anything to try and salvage the marriage, she loved your father more than anything. After our drink, it was time for me to join your father and my other guests downstairs to start our gaming.   Your mother bid everyone goodnight, and headed upstairs to bed."

There was a rap on the door.   Glen waved his hand, and Margo got up to answer.   Two bellmen were there with a tray of sandwiches, and pitchers of lemon water and coffee.   Glen swept everything off of the cluttered coffee table, the men set the refreshments down, and took their leave.   Margo had seen Clarkie and Glenna, sitting on the edge of one of the couches, both waiting for her to sound the alarm so they could pounce on the old man.

"You still with me kiddo?" Margo nodded. Glen poured himself a scotch and continued with his story. "The rest of the weekend is a bit of a blur, we were all drinking so heavily. On that Sunday night, all of my other guests had had enough, so thereafter it was just your father and I. We were playing poker, and the stakes were just getting higher and higher. We had moved our game upstairs to your parents' suite, since it was now just the two of us and the dealer. By early Monday morning, your father owed me so much money that the only way he'd be able to pay would be by signing over his properties...all of them...including his two houses here in New York, and the house that he owned in Savannah, Georgia. In hindsight, I could have just forgiven the debt, but that's not the way underground gambling works, and in those days, we all had our network of thugs to make sure that every debt was paid in full. Just the summer before, there was a gentleman who owned a hotel just like this one in Lake Placid, and didn't want to pay his debt. His hotel mysteriously burned to the ground." Margo was beginning to feel like she might get sick, but put on a smile and continued to listen. "Your mother asked if they could have a few hours to figure everything out, and because of my love for her, I conceded. I left them alone, but three hours later, your father's young lawyer Sam Clark showed up, followed by your grandfather Edward two hours after that. I assumed that your mother had called them as your father was still completely bombed. I went to the suite, where a terrified Sam sat with the deeds to the properties, and a promissory note already signed by your father in hand. I could hear your parents and grandfather screaming in the other room, but couldn't make out the crux of their conversation. I was still very drunk. When their voices quieted, I could actually hear more of what was being said. I heard your mother say, 'I have to do this David, to save us, and our girls. We have no choice.' When they emerged from the other room, Edward took the deeds and promissory note, put them in his pocket, and told me that I would be paid the entire amount, in cash, within twenty four hours. He told me that he would be needing a suite for the night, and I accompanied him to the lobby to set his accommodations up for the night. The following day, everyone departed, and I was paid in cash shortly thereafter as promised." Glen pulled out a yellowed handkerchief and began wiping sweat from his face. He was suddenly very nervous, and his hands shook.

"Three months later, I was shocked to see your mother in the lobby of the hotel with Sam Clark. She was wearing dark sunglasses, a heavy black coat, and had obviously been crying. They asked if we could speak in my office.   Once inside, your mother told me what had happened on that last night of their visit.   She had called Edward to ask if he would put up the cash for David's gambling debt, she couldn't bear the thought of losing everything, her children having no home. When Edward arrived, he made his conditions clear.   He would pay everything, providing that your mother would sleep with him for one night.   He had wanted her ever since the first night he had seen her, when she was a young prostitute.   David would sign over the deeds to his father, so that Edward would have an explanation for the huge withdrawal of cash if your grandmother Ruth asked, and then later Edward would sign everything back over to David.

After much argument, and heated words exchanged, your mother had conceded to the agreement. Your father was devastated, but felt as if there was no other choice. I asked why she and Clarkie were telling me all of this. Your mother said she had come to beg me to never gamble with your father again, and to never speak of that night to anyone. She wanted to protect her family, and her unborn child. You see Margo, your parents had been sleeping in separate rooms for months. Your brother Jacob, is your grandfather Edward's child."

Margo stood, attempted to run toward the door, and passed out on the floor of the old man's suite.

Chapter 21

Margo awoke in a strange room, laying on a couch.   Her head throbbed, and she did her best to make heads or tails of where she was and what had happened.

Her vision was bleary, and she felt shaky and unsteady.   She heard a voice, and recognized it as Clarkie's.   "Damn it Effie, this has gone way too far!   I think you need to get back here, be with these children, and just tell them the truth yourself!   You should have seen poor Margo, thank God she didn't fall flat on her stomach!"   Margo realized that he must be talking to her mother on the phone.   "Mama," she whimpered, but was too dizzy to get up.   "Margo's awake, I have to go.   I'll call you later Effie, but you think about what I've said!"   Margo drifted off to sleep for a few minutes, and when she woke the second time, Clarkie was by her side.   "I want to go back to the lake Sam.   I don't want to spend one more minute in this hotel."   Clarkie was pensive, "Margo, it's six o'clock in the evening, I think we should get you checked out by a doctor, and I think we should just stay put for the night. Glenna has given us this suite for the night, we could even get a doctor to come here if you'd prefer."   Margo sat up, got her bearings, and in a moment, was on her feet.   "I'm fine.   I'm going to the lake whether you drive, or I walk."   They made their way to the lobby and said their goodbyes to Glenna and her staff.   As the valet pulled the car to the entrance, Margo turned to Glenna, "Be good to your father.   Under that rough exterior is a broken heart, one that showed me a great deal of kindness.   Thank you for everything, perhaps we'll meet again under more ideal circumstances."

They rode in silence for the first half hour, Clarkie wondered if Margo would ever speak to him again. She looked out the window, taking in the scenery, tears streaming down her cheeks. She took a wet wipe out of her purse, and washed her face before finally speaking. "Why Clarkie, why? Why couldn't she have just told us the truth? Does she think that there is anything to gain by torturing us in this way? Is this a game to her?" She paused for an answer that didn't come. She raised her voice, "And furthermore, WHERE IN THE HELL IS SHE?" Clarkie let out a deep sigh, "You know that I can't tell you where she is, Margo. I assure you that this is not a game to her. She has so much to lose right now, so much that she's already lost, like…" he stopped himself, he knew he had said too much. "Other than her dignity, and possibly a lot of respect, what else has she lost, Sam? What about us? Our lives have been completely turned upside down! And now I have to tell my poor little brother something so vile…" She threw up her hands and stopped mid sentence. "I don't want to talk anymore Sam, just get me back to my sister and brother."

Far away, separated from everyone she loved, Effie wept bitter tears. "God, please help me. What have I done to this family?" She moaned, rocking herself, sounds emanating from her like an animal caught in a cruel trap. She kept trying to redirect her mind to her children, but the recollection of that terrible night in 1969 kept worming it's way back in. It had been almost thirty years, and yet, if she allowed herself to, she could see it in her mind as if it had happened yesterday.

"Don't do this Effie! I have loved you since the moment I met you, and you know that. Please, don't do this Effie," David had pleaded. Effie would rather have been burned alive than to spend a night with Edward, but she knew that she would need to act brave. The fate of her family rested on her and her decision. "We don't have a choice David. We will lose everything, the girls will lose their home. There's no other option." Effie recalled how she had felt utterly sickened at the thought of allowing her father-in-law to treat her like a prized pig on the auction block. "I'll just kill myself, make it look like an accident, you and the girls can collect my life insurance policy. I'm sure with what we have in checking and savings, I can sign over everything but our house in Savannah to Glen, then once I'm dead, you and the girls could move there!" Effie recalled how her heart sank at the thought of living without

David. "That's not an option," she had said, "you and I are meant to be, predestined before the dawn of time. There isn't a price too grand to pay to honor the love that we share. We have been estranged because of your destructive lifestyle David, now it has threatened to take everything away from our children, but I have never stopped loving you! I will do what I have to do to patch the hole that you've allowed to be ripped in the fabric of our lives." "Effie, please, there has to be another way! There must be something that…" She had cut him off, "There isn't David. I must do this. He'll get a taste of my flesh, this clunky body that I reside in on earth, but he'll never touch my heart or my soul. My heart belongs to you, and my soul belongs to God.   One day this body will rot in the ground, so let him have his way with it if he must."

Edward had been so rough with her, pawing at her, grabbing her as if she were made of leather.   He had whispered in her ear, "Oh, you're such a good little whore, I knew you would be." He smelled putrid, like sweat, whiskey, pipe smoke, and musty laundry.   Effie could almost imagine the smell of sulfur on him, as if he had come straight out of hell.   The part that made her the most ill was that he did not smell or feel like

David, the only man she had ever loved. It had felt like an eternity to her then, but looking back, Edward had finished relatively quickly. While he was grunting, groaning, and spilling his seed inside her, she had turned her head and vomited all over the carpet. Once finished, he rolled onto his back and fell fast asleep. Effie had dressed as quickly as possible, needing to get out of that disgusting room before she gave in to her desire to gut him like a fish in his sleep. While Edward snored away, she stopped long enough to spit in his face before walking out the door.

Effie sat there all alone, unsure of her next move, wondering what this awful truth was going to do to Jacob when he found out. She had always loved and wanted him, from the day she found out she was pregnant. David had suggested an abortion, but she wouldn't hear of it. "We will raise this child as our own David, and I will never think of him as belonging to anyone but you," she had said. Effie picked up the phone, dialed the familiar number. "Liza, Margo knows about Jacob, she found out tonight. I don't want to be alone right now. May I come spend the night with you?"

Chapter 22

When Margo and Clarkie arrived at the campsite, it was after ten o'clock.   They had spent most of the trip in silence, Margo seething with anger, Clarkie nervous and fidgety.   They could see that Sissy and Jacob were on the dock with the lanterns and citronella candles lit, their laughter floating up to the car on the soft summer breeze.   The moon was full and bright, making the ripples in the lake water appear as liquid silver.   Margo collected her items and slammed the door as hard as she could.   Clarkie rolled the window down, "Tread lightly, Margo. Your brother is going to need a gentle touch right now." Walking toward the camper to drop off her things, she flipped him the middle finger, something completely out of character for her. Clarkie couldn't help but laugh as he drove away.

Margo changed into a pair of comfortable shorts and tee shirt, and made her way down to the dock. "Margo! We weren't expecting you until tomorrow." Jacob was smiling, happier than Margo had seen him in a very long time. Margo laughed, "I couldn't bear the thought of you two having fun without me!"   Jacob and Sissy got up to hug their sister.   She hugged Jacob so tightly, it was hard for him to breathe. Tears fell freely down her cheeks.   He pulled away and surveyed her face, "Hey, what happened up there, hon?"   Sissy looked concernedly at her sister, but didn't say a word.   Margo wiped her face, "Go stoke up the fire and get stuff out to make s'mores.   We'll talk later."

In front of the fire with coffee and s'mores in hand, Margo asked, "So what did you two do today?"   Jacob beamed, "We went fishing!   I'd forgotten how much fun it could be to just relax in the boat and fish.   It wasn't really my day for it, but your prissy, uptight sister over there caught two huge bass, which we had for supper." Jacob rubbed his belly, and Sissy laughed.   "Shut up! I am not uptight...okay, at least not so much this week."   All three laughed, enjoying the comradery at the campfire.   Margo noticed that Jacob was, surprisingly, sober and lucid.   She decided that she wouldn't mention it, and thereby jinx it, or ruin the mood.   Sissy blathered on about a conversation she'd had with Jeff on the phone, and how they'd agreed to go to a marriage workshop when she got home. "They're both so happy right now," Margo thought, "how am I supposed to tell them what happened in Lake George?"   She was still pondering this when Jacob said, "Sissy and I are going for a moonlight swim, wanna join us?" She scratched her head, feeling a small lump that she must have acquired when she'd passed out in the hotel. "Yes, that sounds like fun! But I want to call Marcus first, if that's okay with you guys." "Of course," Sissy smiled, "we'll wait for you. The phone is up in the camper on the charger, but you can bring it down here when you're done. That way we'll have it close by in the morning." Jacob stood to his feet, "Do you want me to get you one of the lanterns off of the dock?" "No, thanks. I think the moonlight is enough tonight."

Margo walked quickly up the incline, her anger rising from her toes to her face. She picked up the cordless, and dialed. After four rings, she heard, "Hello?" She braced herself, "Liza, it's Margo. I know that you know where mother is, and you need to give her this message from me. I will tell Jacob the truth about his conception, the awful fact that mother couldn't seem to leave behind a life of whoring. It will break his heart, crush his spirit, and God only knows how he will ever be repaired. But then she has one week to get her ass back here, or she will never see me, or her unborn grandchild again! I know that she's in pain, but setting us up in this sick game of human chess is not the way she should have dealt with it!" Liza stammered, "But honey, your mama is…" Margo cut her off, "I don't care what she is. One week. Period." She hung up the phone and dialed Marcus. She recounted the horrors of the day, and assured him that she was okay. "I'm coming to be with you," he said, sounding more worried than she had ever heard him before. "No, love. Let me figure this all out on my own. We'll be fine here. I don't know why mother did this, but it has made us closer than we've ever been. We'll come out of this crucible, shiny and new, I know that in my heart. I've thrown the ball back in her court, we'll just have to see what her next move will be. I love you, and I'll call you tomorrow." Margo hung up the phone, and took it with her down the incline.

Sissy and Jacob were already in the lake, floating on tubes. Margo tapped her foot on the dock, "I thought you two were going to wait for me!" Jacob laughed, "We couldn't wait. Come on, there's a tube in here for you, too!" Margo made her way down the ladder, and settled into her tube. The cool water seemed to relax some of the stress that she had been holding in her lower back ever since leaving the hotel. She hated to bring gloom and doom to the night, but she knew that her brother and sister were expecting it eventually. "Jacob, I know that it's kind of late, but at some point I think that you and I need to talk about something serious." He smiled, "Sissy, too, right?" She sighed, "Well it's not really about her. It's about you." He looked at Sissy, "Then it's about her too. We're all in this together now. At least that's the way I feel about it." Margo's mouth felt dry. She had said and done things today that were completely out of her element, but this awful truth about Jacob, she had absolutely no idea how she was going to handle it. Jacob seemed to notice her discomfort. "Margo, I'm going to be okay. You have to remember that if you tell me something that hurts me, it's not really you that's hurting me. Don't feel guilty, and don't pity me. I've spent a lifetime feeling sorry for myself, and where has it gotten me?" Margo suddenly felt cold. "I'm going to get out, you guys enjoy yourselves for as long as you want to, I'll be over by the fire."

Sissy and Jacob watched Margo drying off by the fire, and there was something different about her.   Her shoulders were slumped, she had an aura of sadness and defeat surrounding her.   "Part of me wanted to wait until morning, and then find out what happened up there today," Jacob realized he was being a bit loud and lowered his tone, "but whatever it is, it's really eating at her."   Sissy nodded. "Jacob, it's obviously something about you, do you think you can handle it?"   He thought for a moment.   "I don't know if I can handle it, but I can tell you this, judging by the way she looks, she can't handle the weight of it!   It'd be better to make the burden mine."

As Sissy and Jacob dried off by the fire, Margo was doing her level best to not make eye contact with either of them. Jacob sat next to her and took her hand. She lowered her head, and he gently put his fingers under her chin and pulled it up until her tear filled eyes met his. "Margo, tell me." Tears streamed down her face, "Jacob, daddy was not....he was not...." Jacob interrupted, "He was not my real father. I know that Margo. I've known that for a long time. I think that's partly why I have always drank so heavily...to take my mind off of the fact that I don't fit in to this family the same way you two do." Margo was stunned. "How could you have possibly known that? I just found out today!" He sighed, "Do you remember when I was seventeen and I got drunk and went joyriding in dad's car? I hit a parked car and got arrested, remember?"   Both girls nodded their heads.   "Well, when dad came to bail me out of jail, we were in the car on our way home, and he turned to me and said, 'You are NOT my son.'   I think that it's a common statement that parents sometimes say to their children when they are deeply angry, or hurt, but there was just something about the way he said it…I knew that he was telling the truth. He must have seen in my eyes that I knew he was telling the truth, because then he looked scared as hell, and the next day he apologized in his own way. He said, 'Sometimes when we're angry, we say things that we don't mean,' but I knew that what he had said was true, I could see it in his eyes." Sissy blinked hard, "My God Jacob, I'm so sorry! I had no idea!" Jacob chuckled, "And here I thought you knew everything, Siss. What a let down!" Sissy punched him in the shoulder, and they all laughed. "So, I'm assuming Margo, that you're going to tell me that this Glen Cardinal guy had a fling with mom, and he's my real father." Margo rubbed the back of her neck. "You know, I normally wouldn't encourage this, but you both may want to get a beer before I tell you the rest of the story."

Jacob got the chest cooler, pulled it closer to where they were sitting by the fire, and opened a beer. Sissy opened a bottle of chardonnay and poured herself a glass. Margo took a water, and wadded up some ice in a paper towel for her head. They positioned their folding chairs so that they were close together, facing the lake, with Margo in the middle. Margo sighed, "Jacob…your real father is grandpa Edward." Jacob reeled, "No! No frigging way! How would that even be possible?" Margo was frantically searching for words, "Jacob, I….I don't…" He stood up, planning on running, getting away as fast as possible, as if running away would make what Margo had just said suddenly disappear. He saw the pain on Margo's face, and his heart broke for her.   He sat back down, realizing that he was probably too numb to run anyway. Margo began to speak, "Jacob, mother was desperate, she and daddy could have lost everything…"   Slowly, and meticulously she recounted the story that she had been told that day.   Sissy was wide eyed, and no doubt full of thoughts and emotions, but kept her infamous "stone face" on.   Jacob looked at the water, tears rolling down his face in a steady stream, and didn't make a sound. Margo's heart was breaking for her little brother, she would have done anything to erase this whole week, anything to make everything good again.   "Were things EVER good?", she thought silently to herself as she was speaking the evil of the past into the air.   When she had finished, she waited.   She waited for the screaming, the fury, whatever emotions Jacob had pent up in his emotional well were bound to spill out, or so she thought. They didn't.   Jacob quietly stood up and said, "I need to walk around the lake." With that, he finished his beer, opened another, put one unopened bottle in each pocket, and disappeared into the moonlit night.

Chapter 23

Sissy and Margo stayed up into the night, waiting for their brother to return to the camp. "I really hope he's not getting himself wasted, and into a bunch of trouble," Sissy scowled. "He only took three beers with him Sis, and he was walking, how much trouble could he possibly get into? I think he's just blowing off some steam." Secretly, Margo was worried too, but she figured that there was no sense in both of them bouncing negative thoughts off of each other, and getting all worked up. She hadn't told her siblings about the ultimatum she had given Liza for their mother to return in a week, she was guessing that it wouldn't happen anyway. Around three in the morning, they decided they should try to get some sleep, and retired to the tent.   Neither of them actually slept, they both stayed awake, listening to the sounds of the crickets and peepers, praying to hear Jacob come back.

At five thirty, they heard the zipper of the tent flap open, and there was their little brother.   "Come on ladies, the sun is about to rise!   I'll make the coffee!"   He bounced off toward the fire, whistling to himself.   Margo turned to Sissy, "He doesn't look drunk, and for some reason, he's in a really good mood."   Sissy smirked.   "Damn him!   I was kind of hoping he'd come back drunk and pass out so that you and I could get some sleep!"   Both girls laughed, and heard Jacob outside, "Stop fooling around, we'll miss the sunrise!"

On the dock with their fresh coffee, the trio watched in silence as the sky went from red, to orange, to amber, and finally to a gorgeous azure as the bright summer summer sun made it's glorious entrance.

Sissy decided to break the silence.
"What's going on Jacob?   Talk to us,
what are you feeling?"   He sighed.
"You know, ever since that time when I
was a teenager, and somehow knew that
I didn't belong to dad, I guess I always
kind of thought that I belonged to Clarkie.
He's always tried to be a father figure to
me, and I figured maybe it was because
he was my real father.   I've always
thought that he is in love with mom, do
you guys get that vibe too?"   The girls
nodded affirmatively.   "I guess that
although I'm shocked by all of this, the
more I think about it, the more I
understand that the only dad I've ever
had in my life IS Clarkie.   I mean, he
took me to baseball games, helped me
with all of my scouting events, taught me

how to hunt and fish, he was always there while dad was "working".   There's a big part of me that wants to be angry as hell with mom, for creating this whole mess in the first place, but then I feel sorry for her too.   God knows I've made tons of mistakes in my life, and have just been blessed enough that they didn't cause the same web of chaos that mom's mistakes caused.   Last night, after about a thirty minute long pity party, I started to take stock in my life, and realize just how blessed I am!   I've been surrounded by love in spite of the abominable way that I came to be.   This whole, terrible journey has made the three of us so much closer, and opened my eyes to how much of my precious time on earth I have wasted by feeling sorry for myself.   I still carry the

Banks name, and I think it's high time that somebody brings some honor back to the name! I've decided that I'm going to go back to school. I'm going to do what I wanted to do in the first place, and become a nurse. It's time to stop drifting aimlessly, and set down some roots."

Sissy embraced him, "Oh my, our little boy is growing up." "I hate to be a killjoy," Margo added, "but I think that all three of us would benefit from some kind of counseling when all is said and done. Our whole world as we knew it has changed in just under a week's time."

They sat in silence, watching the wonders of nature's painting before them for the better part of an hour. All three were exhausted, not just from the lack of sleep, but from the the emotional "boot camp" that they had all been enduring. Hand in hand, they sat on the dock as a united force. Sissy wondered, had the storm passed, or were they just in the eye of it now? Had their mother played her entire hand, or was she still hiding a wild card or two.

As if on cue, they heard a car pull into the drive at the top of the camp. Clarkie got out and made his way down to the dock with an envelope in his hand. Sissy grimaced, "This can't be good." Clarkie was visibly nervous, but tried to act as casual as possible. "Good morning gang! How's everybody doing?" To the amusement of her siblings, Margo replied, "Cut the crap Clark, what the hell's in the envelope?" Clarkie fidgeted nervously, "This is from your mother, she gave it to me before she left. I was given strict instructions not to let you open it until you had figured out every other secret. I think that what's in this letter is the last few doses of reality she has for you." Jacob used as much tonal sarcasm as he could muster, "Oh, joy! Maybe next we'll find out that mom is her own grandmother or something!"

The three siblings laughed, but Clarkie was somber. "I would like one of you to read this to the other two, out loud. I already know what's in there, and I don't wish to hear it. I'm going to take a walk around the lake. I'll be back in an hour or so." Clarkie walked up the incline, shoulders slumped over, obviously disturbed by whatever was in the letter. Jacob couldn't resist the urge to add some levity to the moment. "Okay girls, let's do this! 'Rock, paper, scissors'?"

Chapter 24

Jacob had initially been joking when he suggested that they play "Rock, Paper, Scissors" to decide who would read the letter, but had lost the game when the girls took him up on the offer. He threw his sweat soaked curls into a ponytail, lit a cigarette, and opened the envelope. The letter inside from Effie, was hand written, with sentences crossed out, others added, and appeared that she had nervously edited it several times.   He began to read out loud:

"Dearest Children, I am writing this letter to you before I depart.   If I were to have waited until after I leave you at the lake to write it, I don't think I'd have the courage. If you are reading this letter, then you have found out some terrible truths about your father and I.   In most instances, I'm sure that you see me as the villain, the liar, the whore.   You must look back on your childhood, remembering all of the times I forced you to go to church, read

the scriptures, and pray, and think that I
am a hypocrite.   I sincerely apologize for
any pain and misery that my life choices
have caused the three of you.   I could go
on and argue that I did what was
necessary, that I played the hand that
was dealt to me, but I won't.   I have to
believe that everything happens for a
reason.   I could have made different
choices, walked a different path, but then
my dears, I wouldn't have the three of you.
Each one of you is a gift from God, my
only solace now that your father is gone.
I could spend another whole lifetime
dealing with my regrets, but four things
that are not on my list of regrets are your
father, and the three of you.   I loved your
father with an all consuming love that can
not be explained in words.   Clarissa, you

were the product of the first spark of that love, Margo the product of the fire that grew.   Jacob, though you may not think so now, you, even more than your sisters, are they epitome of my love for your father.   In my desperation to try to save the man that I loved from his own self destruction, I made a gruesome choice that resulted in your conception.   I have never, and will never, consider any man other than David Banks to be your father. In a roundabout way, David and I created you together just as much as we created your sisters together."   Tears streamed down Jacob's face as he contemplated what he had just read.   He looked at his sisters' tear stained faces, and read on:

"I'm sure that there are still some loose ends, some things that the three of you have questions about, and I will try to answer the most obvious ones for you now. Yes Jacob, Edward and your father David both knew that biologically you belong to Edward. Unfortunately, so does Ruth. She sees me as the woman who stole her son, and then her husband, though I am neither. I am the woman who loved her son so deeply, that I would allow myself be defiled by her husband, to save her son from destruction. Ruth was told by Edward that we had a drunken affair when he came to help your father financially, she does not know that I was simply one of the chips that Edward placed on the table. You may have noticed that Ruth took ownership of our home in Rochester, and that's because she didn't want us anywhere near her. The only grandchild that she could bear the sight of was Margo. I'm sure that if you contacted her during this time for information, she was not kind. I don't blame her, though I wish she had all of the facts, all of the information. Maybe even then she wouldn't understand. If you children are angry with me for keeping these secrets for all of these years, I truly apologize, but here are a couple more to add to your collection. Six years ago, I was diagnosed with breast cancer. A few months later, I was told that the cancer was spreading to other parts of my body, and was now in my bones. I pondered how I was going to break the news to the three of you for a couple of more months after that.   At that time, I told your father that I was going to sit down with the three of you, and lay the whole truth out to you- my cancer, my past, everything.   He tried to forbid it, and when I wouldn't yield, he took his own life by overdosing in our home.   He couldn't bear the thought of the three of you knowing the dirty details of our lives, and being left behind alone to deal with it after I passed.   As fate would have it, you children were all in other states when your father committed suicide, which made it easier to sell the heart attack story to you.   With Clarkie's help, I was able to get your father's death record sealed, and convince everyone that he had died of a heart attack, including your grandmother Ruth.   Ruth is fond of telling people that he actually died of a broken heart caused by me, little does she know that although she says it to be spiteful, it is absolutely true.

As you read this letter, I am at our home in Savannah, GA. Only Clarissa has ever seen this home, and she was too young to remember it. This is the only place I have ever felt truly at home, so it seemed natural to return here at this point in my life. The memories here are all good ones, your father and I were so in love, a team and united front when we lived in this house. Your father's remains are here with me in an urn.   The plot that you've all visited in Rochester is the home of an empty coffin.   I did that for your grandmother Ruth.   My heart told me that I needed to bring your father home, so his remains have been here for the last five years.   If I had known then what I know now, maybe we would have never left this place, but then as I've said before, everything happens for a reason. Had we not left here, I wouldn't have had Jacob.   I wish that you could have met my people, Jacob, you take after them a great deal.   I have not had contact with them in many years, but if you ever wanted to, I should think that it would not be too hard to find your Solomon cousins in Natchez.

To answer another question that may be on your minds, yes, I have been trying to treat my cancer.   In the last six years, I have tried every treatment available to me, but I believe all that they have done is buy me some time.   Hiding my illness has been a chore, one that I am ready to lay down at this point.   I have had help from outsiders keeping my cancer from becoming public knowledge, and I owe a great debt to a lady here named Trudy, who does all of my wigs and hairpieces and sends them to me.   I'm sure as you all hug me goodbye today, not one of you will notice that I am wearing a wig.   I smoke a little marijuana every now and again, to help ease my nausea, and make it possible for me to eat.   The wigs, the marijuana, the lying, none of it will be necessary any longer.   Scans show that my cancer has spread to my brain, and I have decided to stop all artificial treatment, all efforts to look "normal", and enjoy as much time as possible here.

When I left you at the lake, children, I spoke of your inheritance.   Clarkie will be able to release those funds to you, minus a small amount for me to live on until the day comes when I cross over to be with your father.   My body will be cremated, all arrangements have already been paid for, so you needn't worry about having to deal with that later.   I hope that my decision to have the three of you join together at the lake was the right one. I did it, because I knew that it would bring the three of you closer together. My best memories of the three of you as children all come from our times at the lake property.

I want you all to return to your respective homes now, please don't come here to find me. I am spending time here in solace with your father, and Liza is always near when I need her. Jacob, you may live in my house there if you'd like, it will be yours as of today anyway.

Once you are all home and settled, I will contact the three of you by phone. Beyond that, I've decided that when I know the end is near, I would like to come back, and spend my last days with you, my dear children, at the lake property. My prayer is that the three of you will have forgiven me, and will be willing to come back to spend those last few precious moments with me.   I love you Clarissa, Margo, and Jacob.   Nothing could or ever will change that.   Be good to each other, be good to yourselves."

She had ended the letter abruptly, not even so much as adding "Love, Mom" at the end.   Tears flowed freely in the Banks camp.   The children were all in deep mourning, mostly for the life they thought they had known.   Now, the puzzle was complete, and they would all have to go home and try to forge a normal life out of the rubble that Effie had left them in.   Sissy wiped her eyes and said, "I remember that when we were children and used to squabble, mother would say 'one day, your father and I will be gone, and all you children will have left is each other'.   I guess that was one thing she was telling the truth about."

Afterward

Clarkie stood at the edge of the lake, pondering what he had allowed his life to become. He had been friend, counselor, mediator, henchman, and confidant to the Banks family for more years than he could recall. He had become a lawyer with essentially one client. He thought of the brilliant career he had envisioned in his youth, with dazzling, heated moments in courtrooms, trials that would put him on the covers of papers, fame, fortune, a trophy wife, and perfect family. All of this he had traded to serve the Banks family. He had allowed himself to fall in love with Effie, and that love had kept him doing all of her and David's dirty work long after he had tired of it. "Maybe now, I will retire and travel the country," he thought to himself. He knew in his heart that this was a foolish dream. He would need to work and stay busy, so as not to be overcome by a lifetime of memories, especially the memory that he would have of today. The sound of the leaves rustling in the cool October breeze broke his train of thought, and he decided that it was time to go.

He made his way up the incline, and then turned back around to look at the lake.   Mother nature had fashioned an exquisite portrait around the lake, in hues of green, gold, orange, and crimson. The afternoon sun played off of the crystal lake, and the slight ripples animated the reflection of the gorgeously painted leaves on the surface.   He looked at the four empty Adirondack chairs on the dock, and replayed the images of what he had witnessed just two short hours ago.

Late that morning, Effie had announced that she knew today was the day she would make her final journey, leave her mortal shell.   The children had all come the day before, at her request.   Margo had asked, "Mama, what would you like us to do for you?"   Effie had responded, "I want to sit on the dock with the three of you.   I don't want to die here in this camper."   The hospice nurse, who had been there to keep Effie comfortable, administered one last dose of oral morphine before taking her leave.   Sissy and Jacob had wheeled Effie to the dock in her wheelchair, and transferred her to one of the chairs.   The urn with David's remains was in her lap.   The three children had taken their places in the other chairs, Margo holding her brand new swaddled baby.   She had named him Solomon in honor of her mother's family.

"I'm so proud of all three of you," Effie had said, "I can't imagine having been in your shoes. There were so many terrible moments in my life, but I always had choices to make. The three of you were not given that luxury, you were forced to deal with the aftermath of the choices that I made. I hope above all, that you have learned something valuable from me. A life lived in the shadows is no life at all. I have really only felt alive for these last three months, finally free of my self imposed prison. It's quite ironic, that now as I sit here dying, I feel so full of life. This cancer, I believe, was created and nurtured by my own bitterness, my own deceit. Don't feel sorry for me, for when this life is over, I will be truly free. Clarissa, continue to work on your relationship with Jeff. It's obvious to me that the two of you deeply love one another. I have no doubt in my mind that when I cross today, I will meet the spirit of your children who are yet to be conceived. Margo, your sweet spirit has always been your greatest asset, but I believe that the experience the three of you had here this summer has shown you that you have the strength of an ox as well! Teach that baby, and any others that follow, that true happiness comes from knowing and accepting who we really are, and that true strength comes from love, not hate. Jacob, what can I say? This summer was the summer that you truly became a man. I'm so glad that you've decided to chase after the dream that you've had for yourself, forsaking whatever mold your father tried to put you in. You will be a fantastic nurse, and I have no doubt in my mind that you will also one day be a great husband, and father." The children had seen that she was losing her strength, and surrounded her chair to place their hands on her, comfort her in these last moments. She had opened her mouth to speak one last time, "I love all...", and then she was gone. The children had wept, but there was more hope than sadness in their hearts. Jacob had looked up into the sky and said, "See you later, mama." After the funeral home had sent a van, and collected Effie's body, the three siblings embraced one another on the dock. The book had been closed, a new one waiting to be written. Clarkie had been asked to hold Solomon after Effie had passed, and couldn't help but think that he could see a glimpse of her in his tiny face.

Clarkie blinked his eyes, setting aside the images that had just replayed in his mind. There it was again, a beautiful and haunting portrait, bordered by the beauty of the lake…four empty chairs on the end of the dock.

The Banks of the Lake

The Banks Family Saga

By Andrew Charles

Table of Contents

Made in the USA
Lexington, KY
24 January 2017